# HEAT FOR SALE

by

LETA BLAKE

An Original Publication from Leta Blake Books

Published as Blake Moreno by Dark Ink in 2018

Heat for Sale Written by Leta Blake
Cover by Dar Albert
Formatted by BB eBooks



First Print Edition, 2018
ISBN 978-1-626226-48-7

# Other Books by Blake Moreno

## Contemporary

Will & Patrick Wake Up Married
Will & Patrick's Endless Honeymoon
Cowboy Seeks Husband
The Difference Between
Bring on Forever
Stay Lucky

**Sports**

The River Leith

*The Training Season Series*
Training Season
Training Complex

**Musicians**

Smoky Mountain Dreams
Vespertine

**New Adult**

Punching the V-Card

**Winter Holidays**

*The Home for the Holidays Series*
Mr. Frosty Pants
Mr. Naughty List
Mr. Jingle Bells

## Fantasy

Any Given Lifetime

**Re-imagined Fairy Tales**

Flight
Levity

**Paranormal & Shifters**

Angel Undone
Omega Mine

**Horror**

Raise Up Heart

## Omegaverse

*Heat of Love Series*
Slow Heat
Alpha Heat
Slow Birth
Bitter Heat

*For Sale Series*
Heat for Sale
Bully for Sale

## Coming of Age

*'90s Coming of Age Series*
Pictures of You
You Are Not Me

## Audiobooks

Leta Blake at Audible

## Discover more about the author online

Leta Blake
letablake.com

## Gay Romance Newsletter

Leta's newsletter will keep you up to date on her latest releases and news from the world of M/M romance. Join the mailing list today and you're automatically entered into future giveaways.

## Leta Blake on Patreon

Become part of Leta Blake's Patreon community in order to help support her in the production of books and audiobooks. Access deleted scenes, extras, bonus stories, interviews, and early chapters. www.patreon.com/letablake

## Acknowledgments

Thank you to the following people:

B & C for being my everythings. Mom & Dad without whom I couldn't follow my passion for writing. Thanks to all the wonderful members of my Patreon who inspire, support, and advise me, especially Sadie Sheffield. Thank you to Einat and Neta for beta reading and their excellent suggestions. Thanks to Amanda Jean for the editing work and to DJ Jamison for proofing. Thank you to Daphne du Maurier for the inspiration. Thank you to my sister-in-law Cindy for additional inspiration via a passing comment one day.

And, most especially, thank you to all my readers who always make the blood, sweat, and tears of writing worthwhile.

In a world where omegas sell their heats for profit, Adrien is a university student in need of funding. With no family to fall back on, he reluctantly allows the university's matcher to offer his virgin heat for auction online. Anxious, but aware this is the reality of life for all omegas, Adrien hopes whoever wins his heat will be kind.

Heath—a wealthy, older alpha—is rocked by the young man's resemblance to his dead lover, Nathan. When Heath discovers Adrien is Nathan's lost son from his first heat years before they met, he becomes obsessed with the idea of reclaiming a piece of Nathan.

Heath buys Adrien's heat with only one motivation: to impregnate Adrien, claim the child, and move on. But their undeniable passion shocks him. Adrien doesn't know what to make of the handsome, mysterious stranger he's pledged his body to, but he's soon swept away in the heat of the moment and surrenders to Heath entirely.

Once Adrien is pregnant, Heath secrets him away to his immense and secluded home. As the birth draws near, Heath grows to love Adrien for the man he is, not just for his connection to Nathan. Unaware of Heath's past with his omega parent and coming to depend on him heart and soul, Adrien begins to fall as well.

But as their love blossoms, Nathan's shadow looms. Can Heath keep his new love and the child they've made together once Adrien discovers his secrets?

*Heat for Sale* is a stand-alone m/m romance by Leta Blake. Infused with a *Rebecca*-style secret, it features a well-realized omegaverse, an age-gap, dominance and submission, heats, knotting, and scorching sex scenes.

For Rebecca

# PART ONE

## Heat

*In a world where omegas are treated as second-class citizens, and their precious heats are contracted and sold, they have little protection except a flimsy consent law that's rarely enforced.*

*Poor omegas can auction their heats off to the highest bidder. Should a breeding be negotiated as part of the heat contract, and if a baby is conceived, an omega must live with his new alpha for the full term of the pregnancy—four months—in order to have steady access to gestation stabilizing compounds only the alpha can provide him.*

*The dual biological drives of heat and pregnancy keep these men together for the short term, but while all contracts end with an exchange of money, not all end in love.*

# Chapter One

ADRIEN PACED BY the window of his dorm room with his cell phone pressed to his ear. He'd known it was coming. Every omega did, but somehow between his day-to-day studies and his research into Hontu tribal materials, he'd managed to forget about it most of the time. But Ron Finch, his university's professional matcher, had removed any ambiguity about the matter. With a firm and undeniable voice, he'd made it quite clear: the time had come for Adrien to sell his first heat.

All omegas faced this moment, but most of them had family to rely on to help them make a good choice. For better or for worse, Adrien was alone in the world, so the decision of how to proceed with regards to his heat was entirely up to him.

"Review the options again?" Sweat pooled in the small of his back, despite the room's roaring air conditioner. Adrien wiped at his face, finding his upper lip and forehead damp.

"The first option, and the most popular by far, is to have a family member arrange for the purchase of your first heat by some well-to-do friend or business associate. Since your father, God rest his soul, has passed on to the next world, and you don't know the whereabouts of the omega who birthed you, the duty could reasonably fall to an uncle or brother."

"No," Adrien gritted out, his glasses slipping down a bit on his nose. "I have no family."

"In that case, the second option is to allow me, as matcher of the university, to see if there are any alphas amongst the alumni who'd like to purchase your heat outright. Obviously, the university takes a small percentage of the price as a fee for service rendered. I admit, though, Adrien, given your financial situation, the third option might be the best one for you. It's guaranteed to generate the greatest profit for your valuable and once-in-a-lifetime first heat."

"And what's that entail?" He already knew, but he needed to hear it again to make it real.

"An online public auction of the heat. Ninety percent of the proceeds go to you and ten percent go to the university for the trouble. If you want, we could offer an attempt at breeding you at a premium. That will bring in the highest possible bids. Obviously, there are alumni of the university who'll pay a tidy sum when offered a heat purchase directly, but if you give them an omega to bid on? Especially one as handsome as you? Well, they'll bankrupt themselves in a frenzy of competition for the right to claim your first heat. And, if you're willing, they'll shell out even more for a chance at breeding you."

Adrien ran a hand over the flat, toned stomach beneath his soft sweater. He cleared his throat, words stuck for a moment, until he finally said, "I'm not sure I'm ready to try for a pregnancy."

"Understandable. But you have to also consider your finances. Certainly you can sell future heats and breeding attempts, but none will go for so high a price as a first heat and first breeding combined. You know how much alphas like to stake their claims—even if it is only for a single season."

Adrien closed his eyes. He'd face up to ten such 'seasons' in his life. No omega had been known to go into heat more than ten times, and most averaged only five, but each successive season was less fertile than the last and brought in less money. Assuming you didn't fall in love with an alpha and marry him. Then one man handled all an omega's seasons and became financially responsible for his well-being for life. Such pairings were common but not expected.

"And, as you know, unless you fall for one another, which is highly unlikely, any child you bear is the concern of the alpha. You wouldn't be required to participate in its life at all. The wee thing would be immediately transferred to the alpha's care after a period of chestfeeding and then weaning."

"That's still a large portion of my life. Four months of pregnancy followed by a year of chestfeeding, at a minimum. The interruption to my college career would be a strain." To put it mildly. He'd only just begun to really make headway understanding the connection between Hontu woven fabric and their spiritual life.

"College can wait," Mr. Finch said. "I see in your files your goal is to be named a certified art history professor. For you, an omega, to have that chance the government demands a large fee. According to your university accounts, you're barely able to afford another year of education, and I'm not even sure if you can achieve enough funds to reach your goal. Even by selling the breeding along with the heat."

Adrien's stomach hurt.

"But, if you truly want to aim for such a lofty future career, then an online, public auction is definitely the only chance you've got."

"Do I have to decide now? About the breeding, I mean?"

"So it'll be the auction for sure?"

"Yes, as you point out, I have no other choice financially."

Mr. Finch made a happy sound. "Excellent. We can always get the auction going with just the first heat on offer. Once the pot is bubbling with bids, we can sweeten it by offering the breeding as an add-on. It always creates a frenzy to drop the breeding offer mid-auction. Drives the alphas wild."

Adrien's head swam. He sat down on the hard single bed he'd slept on for the last four years of studies. "What do I have to do? What's the next step?"

"You'll come to my offices tomorrow. We'll discuss the protocol for provoking your first heat. Then you'll pose for some photos for the auction—naked, of course, so they can see the goods. Make sure to have everything down there looking as nice as possible. A little trimming never hurt anyone! It can actually help make the package look a bit bigger. After that I'll work up the wording for the online auction, set it up for you, and get it started immediately. We'll be able to sense within the first day whether or not we need to be worried."

Adrien's mouth went dry. "Why would we need to worry?"

"In your case, based on the photos in your file, I think you'll be fine. You're young and attractive, though that mop of blond hair could be a bit neater. Stereotypically, alphas do prefer brunets, fair or not. Still, there are always the fetishists who love the lighter hair. You have a tender look about you, and that will make them want to take you apart," the matcher said, a hint of laughter in his voice. "And when you're in heat, you'll *want* him to take you apart, too. Ah, heat. It makes sluts of us all."

Adrien shuddered.

Would he be a slut in heat? He couldn't imagine wanting a stranger to touch him, take him, and impregnate him. But the matcher was right; he was running low on the funds his father had left to him when he died. And without family to fall back on, he was definitely in a place in life where he had little choice but to go the auction route. While he dreaded the thought of carrying a stranger's child, of interrupting his studies and his student life so thoroughly, he also knew he'd likely have to agree to be bred, too.

If he was very lucky, in a best-case scenario, he'd auction off the breeding for high value, but it wouldn't take. That way he'd collect all the breeding money without having to pay the ultimate price of time, discomfort, and pain.

Still, he wasn't ready to admit any of that aloud just yet. It would make it too real.

Pacing the floor of his small dorm room, he agreed to let the matcher set up the auction and make the appointment for him to come into the office the next day for photographs. After a week or so, he'd give his consent to offer up his first breeding, too.

He rubbed his eyes beneath his glasses. They stung with sweat. It couldn't be that bad. Every omega did it. He'd be just like anyone else.

He just wished he didn't have to be.

# Chapter Two

THE MATCHER'S OFFICE was garishly decorated and reminded Adrien of a brothel in a movie, complete with red curtains and wallpaper to match. Mr. Finch himself was unattractive enough—short, stubby, and stinking of cigar. He'd been on his cell phone when Adrien first arrived, but he'd waved him into a chair across from his wide wooden desk and smiled. Then he'd swung his feet up on top, leaned back, and lit a cigar, puffing it at the ceiling. A nameplate resting on the front of the desk read *Ron Finch*.

"I know, Phil, but this one is a doozy of an omega, I tell you. He's hungry for cash, and you know what that means." Ron winked at Adrien and flicked his ash in the red tray on his desk. "He's here now. Yes, he's handsome. Plus he has a sexy little butt that jiggles just right when he walks. I'm telling you, it's worth putting up a fight for him. You'll see."

Adrien swallowed back bile and squirmed in his seat.

Ron didn't seem to care or notice. "Now, don't forget to brag to your friends. They'll all want to make you sweat for him, I'm sure." Ron chuckled and then hung up the phone. "Chumming the water for you, Adrien. Getting the sharks hungry."

Adrien smiled, but there was no joy in it. "Thanks."

"So, first, let's review how we'll trigger your heat. Once the auction closes, you'll have a week and a half before your heat will need to start. During that time, you'll be prescribed two hormones that will force your heat forward. Future heats will give warning signs several months in advance. Those signals are best not ignored if you want to capitalize on them."

"Sell them, you mean."

"Exactly. So long as you're a student or professor here at the university, I can help you sell those heats, or, once I've retired, whoever takes my place can help. If you marry, however, that alpha will be responsible for dealing with the heat. Of course, some married omegas do continue to sell their heats for profit in order to benefit their entire family, but we usually stay out of that and let the alpha handle those arrangements."

Adrien pushed his glasses up his nose and nodded.

"And, obviously, some older omegas take up the duty of selling their heats themselves on less than reputable sites or in individual transactions. We advise you to stay away from that if possible. You have a stellar matching service here at the university, so you should absolutely take advantage of it."

There wasn't any new information in Ron's little speech, but it made Adrien feel a bit better to hear it all spelled out, and he was glad for any reason to stall for time on the photos.

But it seemed as though his time was up.

Ron stubbed out his cigar. "Now, let's get started with the pictures. I have a room here where I take them. I try to keep them all in the same tone so no one can accuse me of favoritism. Though if I had a current favorite among the heats up for sale, it would be you." He smiled at Adrien and winked.

Adrien cringed. "How do the pictures…? I mean, what will I have to do for them?" Adrien knew that auctions were conducted for campus omegas' heats on a regular basis, but he'd never taken a look at the website himself. He'd been too afraid of what he might see of his future there.

"It's easy, really. Naked, hands crossed behind the back for the first shot. I'll take a lot of those just to make sure I capture you with the most appealing expression on your face. It helps to show subservience in your eyes if possible. That can be hard for some omegas to accomplish, but I think you'll be a natural. Then I take that same pose from behind. That frames the buttocks, which, as you know, is every alpha's obsession." He laughed. "After that, I'll grab one of you bent over with cheeks spread so they can see your anus. Finally, I'll snap a few of just your face. Again, aiming to capture one with the right mix of innocence, desire, and a hint of fear. And that'll do it." He dusted off his hands to indicate a finished product. "And, let me tell you, son, if you've got a nice-looking hole, you'll see the bids jump as soon as I load the pictures to the site. Alphas love a tight, young anus."

Ignoring the pounding of his heart, Adrien said, "Bids have already started?"

"Absolutely. I put the auction live last night after our conversation with a write-up about you. Alphas are always looking for an intelligent omega to breed, you know. It's not just about looks. They don't want stupid offspring who won't bring any glory to the family name. So your GPA alone was enough to get some takers."

"But I thought we weren't going to offer breeding just yet?"

"We haven't!" Ron waved Adrien's concern away. "I made sure to mention that you wanted to be a professor. When the early-bidding alphas saw you were ambitious as well as intelligent, they started out with higher bids than usual, rightly assuming that you'd be offering up breeding in the end. The wealthier alphas especially want to make sure their children have some drive to take over their businesses or fortunes once they're retired or passed on." Ron grinned.

Adrien noted for the first time that Ron's teeth were crooked. He couldn't tell if Ron was a beta or an omega himself, but he knew he definitely wasn't an alpha.

"How high have the bids gone?" Adrien asked, his heart pounding harder.

"Don't you fret about numbers yet," Ron said. "After I post the pictures, the bids will shoot way up. Because, yes, intelligence matters, but alphas are ignited by a sexy body and a pretty face. You're going to make them cream their pants just imagining having the first go at you. And when you offer breeding after a few days' time, oh, the fight will be on. Bids will absolutely skyrocket."

Heat pooled in Adrien's stomach. A weird sense of pride at the idea of potentially commanding a high price warred with the inherent disgust that swamped him whenever he thought of selling his body in this way. He focused on his earlier question, the one Ron had waved off. "Why are the alphas who want to breed bidding on me when I haven't offered it yet? What makes them so sure?"

"Oh, they know the name of the game," Ron said cheekily. "They figure even if you don't offer it, they can probably convince you in the throes of heat to take on a breeding for less than the price you'd demand if you were putting it on the table right now."

A rancid bile rose in Adrien's throat. "That's not fair, though. Omegas don't think clearly in heat."

Ron raised a thin brow. "And that's exactly what they're counting on. Let's put it this way: the world ain't fair, pretty pauper. But you won't have to worry about that because you're going to offer the breeding beforehand. Now, let's get your glasses and clothes off and take those pictures."

The process of being photographed was humiliating. As Adrien walked back to his dorm, evading the eyes of his fellow students, he wondered how many of them had gone through the same ordeal. It was hard to tell an omega from a beta, since those sexes appeared so outwardly similar and were only inwardly different. Alphas, however, were easy to pick out. They had a certain swagger and were typically larger than betas and omegas. Adrien could identify them at a distance.

As he hustled down the busy sidewalks, he found himself trying to guess at the sex of each person he passed. He wondered if those he suspected of being omegas had already had their first heat and how they'd dealt with it all. The alphas didn't make eye contact with him, which was nothing new, but he found himself darting glances their way, curious about whether any of them had handled an omega in heat before.

He grimaced as an alpha with a thickly muscled neck lifted a brow when he caught Adrien looking. He ducked his head and hurried onward, not wanting to invite attention. Still, he had so many questions. What was a heat like for an alpha? He knew it was profoundly pleasurable—that was why they were willing to bid on omegas so steeply—but he also knew they didn't feel as out of control as an omega, keeping their head for the majority of the heat. But he sometimes wondered if handling a heat changed how alphas viewed all omegas afterward.

Seeing a man so undone, so out of control and lost in his lust, taking care of him, and catering to his urgent and overpowering needs…did some alphas stop considering an omega to be fully human after that experience? Is that what led so many of them to resist the changes in omega voting rights and professional certificates?

And what about the omegas who went through these heats? A heat like he was going to be in very soon? Adrien swallowed hard, pushing down the surge of fear. How humiliating would it be to go so entirely feral, to be needy beyond measure, and to be broken down like that in front of an alpha who knew nothing else about him?

Adrien wiped a hand over his upper lip. How was he ever going to get through a heat with a stranger? He'd been so embarrassed to have Ron take pictures of his asshole. It'd been horrifying. His eyes pricked and burned. Would the shame of bending over and spreading his cheeks for Ron—squat and smoking as he bent over with his camera—pale in comparison to what he was about to face? He didn't see how it wouldn't. He'd have to do so much more with whatever alpha won him for his first season.

Just thinking of Ron's contented sigh when he'd spotted Adrien's hairless scrotum and bare hole made him feel cold inside. And the way Ron had praised him, saying, "That's a delicious little pucker. The alphas will want to eat you up," had Adrien's small omega-testicles trying to climb up into his body.

"Hey, Adrien!"

Adrien groaned and quickened his step on the sidewalk. Maybe he could pretend not to have heard. Lance was the last person he wanted to see right now. And he didn't see him, actually. The crowd around them was thick, and his eyes were on the sidewalk. He had plausible deniability.

Not only was Lance his research assistant in the art history department, and thus his underling, but he was also a happy-go-lucky omega with another year and a half at least before he'd have to face his first season. Wealthy and connected, Lance would entertain a completely different situation than Adrien. His father had already sold the rights to his son's first heat to a friend of the family, a man Lance had crushed on since childhood. There would be no humiliating public online auction for him. Money had its privileges.

"Wait up!" Lance's voice called out, but Adrien hurried on, pretending obliviousness.

The idea of telling Lance what he'd just been through with Ron and the necessary photographs filled him with boiling, frothy shame. He wondered if there was any way to keep all of this to himself for as long as possible. Maybe, when the time came, he could just tell Lance and the others in the department that he was taking a vacation, instead of confessing to everyone that he was off to have his heat handled.

In a stroke of luck, a crowd of students burst out of his dormitory building just as he reached it, separating him from Lance's long-legged advance. Adrien ducked inside and took the empty stairwell rather than risking crossing the busy lobby to take the elevator up to his hall. He didn't want to run into anyone he knew and field an awkward conversation, nor did he want to give Lance the opportunity to catch up with him.

He just wanted to be alone to process.

Safe inside his dorm room, he sat down, shaky and sick, in front of his computer. He had to see the truth for himself. He had to know. With clammy hands, he typed in the address of the university's omega auction site and sat back in his seat, fingers pressed over his mouth.

There on the front page under the heading NEW AND FRESH was his listing. He stared at the photos that Ron must have loaded as soon as he'd left the office. His asshole was there on the internet for the whole world to see. His own white hands held his ass cheeks apart and revealed it like a secret he'd kept and never wanted exposed.

His entire body flashed hot and then cold, before going so hot again that he felt sweat slipping down the side of his face. He stared at the photo of his face. In it, his eyes glimmered with unshed tears, and his cheeks flushed with his embarrassment. His full mouth was slightly open and looked obscenely red.

*Creamy, pink skin!* read one of Ron's captions. *These sweet buns are worth grabbing!* read another. Adrien shuddered. Apparently, this was what being an omega really meant: being nothing more than a product to sell.

The rest of the write-up was similar:

*Adrien is an intelligent omega with a beautiful body, a focused mind, and a pleasant personality. An excellent student with a near-perfect GPA, his goal is to become a professor here at our very own university. Needless to say, a good return on his first heat would go a long way toward making that possible for him.*

*Adrien's is a special kind of beauty. Notice the fine hairs on his buttocks. Though blond, they shimmer beautifully in the light. His fleshy ass begs to be gripped and one can easily imagine how nicely it will bounce with an alpha's deep thrusts. His skin is pale, yes, but will flush attractively in the throes of heat.*

"Painting a picture, creating a fantasy is an important aspect of my work," Ron had said while he took picture after picture. "And I know just what I'll say about you."

Adrien tucked his lower lip into his mouth, chewing it anxiously, and read on. His eyes flew wide at the next words.

*Adrien is untouched. A virgin in every way. Oh, lucky alpha, you'll be winning more than just his first heat.*

How had Ron known that? Did he have access to Adrien's health files? He must. The only person Adrien had confessed his virginity to was the nurse he'd seen for his regular checkup, and only because it was part of the questionnaire he'd been asked to fill out for his heat risk assessment.

Shaking, he allowed himself to scroll down, heart in his throat and fingers trembling. The number at the bottom indicated the current highest bid was greater than he'd feared but far less than he'd hoped. What if he did this and didn't even get enough to pay for his school, much less the government's fee to become a certified professor? He buried his head in his hands.

He shouldn't have looked.

After a few long minutes, he lifted his head, noted the highest bid had gone up, but just barely, and closed down the site. Then he clicked open his research files on Hontu dyes and fabrics instead. He had work to do and continuing to fret about something he couldn't control wasn't going to change that.

What choice did he have? His first season was coming, and he had a heat to sell. There was no shame in it. Every omega faced these kinds of choices.

As he began to reorganize some of his most recent research notes, he scoffed under his breath. "Tell that to my ears." They continued to burn hot every time he remembered the way his eyes had met Ron's camera lens and the resulting image he'd glimpsed online. In it, he'd looked scared, exposed, and vulnerable.

Probably because that was exactly what he was.

# Chapter Three

HEATH STARED AT the photo of the boy on the auction page. He didn't usually look for heats to bid on, but his friend, Felix, had been bragging about holding the top bid on the newest boy offered by their shared alma mater's matcher. When Felix had described the boy's looks as being very like Heath's own beloved Nathan's, his curiosity had gotten the better of him.

And now he was hooked.

The ripe, slightly open mouth combined with the blond hair, almond-brown eyes, and high cheekbones did remind him rather intensely of Nathan, the only omega he'd ever made the mistake of loving. And losing. In the darkest hours of the night, he still tried to convince himself that Nathan had loved him in return. He'd only had five years with his beloved before he'd died from a previously undiagnosed fatal flaw in his heart, but they had been years of such intensity that Heath was still reeling from them. Memories of Nathan, along with pain, rose up in him again, raw and aching.

*Shattering grin. Mischievous eyes. A penchant for trouble.*

Good God, Nathan had brought Heath to his knees again and again, and then died there in his arms. Tragic, in every damn way. But alongside the pain came a beating pulse of desire for the boy in the photograph. Certainly, though, the lust had little to nothing to do with the boy himself and everything to do with Heath's memories of Nathan squirming beneath him in the throes of ecstatic heat.

Felix had been right. The resemblance was so strong, so fantastic, that Heath lost his breath counting the similarities. As he continued to study the photos of Adrien, his mind slowly unraveled.

A tangle of feelings and memories, half-formed plans, and calculations possessed him. If the boy in the photos was twenty, as stated in the auction ad, then that would correspond with what Heath remembered of Nathan's recounting of his first breeding. The one he'd auctioned off when he was still in school. Nathan had been won by an older alpha with kind eyes—that was how he always described him—and he'd given the child up to the alpha father as agreed in advance so that he could continue his schooling. After graduating with a degree in dance and theater, Nathan had used the bonus pregnancy money he'd earned to travel the world. It was only two years after that he and Heath had met at a party in the artsy city of Waterston in the Northern Province, both of them young and intoxicated. Nathan had flashed that charming smile, and Heath had been quick to fall in love.

Heath tilted his head and examined the photos of Adrien, wondering what the boy looked like when he smiled. The resemblance was too great and the timing much too uncanny. Quick calculations told Heath that Nathan would have been just barely twenty-one when this omega, Adrien, was born.

He clicked through to the private, bidders-only pedigree page, with details of parentage kept secret even from the omegas themselves, to look into Adrien's ancestry. His pulse thundered wildly. This boy who stared at him from the screen with fear and trepidation, and with such beautiful tears glistening in his eyes, *was* Nathan's son. His entire legal name was given as birth omega with absolute certainty, and if there had been any doubt, Heath recognized Nathan's signature on all of the contracts and forms. Not to mention the birth certificate was stamped as PRIVATE SEALED FOR ALPHA USE ONLY, as Nathan had assured him whenever Heath had asked about the likelihood of his child ever finding him.

"Darling, he's never going to find me, even if he looks. The files are sealed from the world until his heat begins, assuming he's even an omega. And then only his potential alphas will have the right to the information. If they choose to tell him, well..." Nathan had shrugged. "It's not as though I'll be under any obligation to meet him. I did my duty."

Heath stared at Adrien's picture again. He was beautiful.

A living, breathing piece of Nathan...

Just how similar was he exactly? Would he sound like Nathan? Would he cry out the same way, or beg, or glance over his shoulder while being fucked with the same smug gaze? Would he tease and withhold and torment Heath as Nathan always had?

Or would he let Heath breed him like Nathan never allowed? Could Heath fill him with a child? A thrill shuddered through him. That child would be a genetic piece of Nathan to hold onto, to cherish. He could breed this Adrien omega and have everything he ever wanted. Or almost.

Heath licked his lips and adjusted his cock.

The offer for breeding wasn't on the table yet. But given the write-up about Nathan's son—intelligent, ambitious, with the goal to be an art history professor—the breeding would be offered up soon. Heath knew how much it cost to pay the government fee for an omega to be named a professor. He'd paid it himself once upon a time, though he'd only paid the lower cost of an alpha certification. Omegas were charged much more.

That had been a long time ago, and the price had only gone up. After giving up his professorial title to take his inherited place in the peerage, Heath had retired to his house in the city to read books, entertain other peers, manage his familial estates, handle his useless brother and nephew, fuck Nathan, and drink. After Nathan's death, he'd added more of the other five to make up for his loss.

Heath cleared his throat and glanced down at the highest bid still held by his friend Felix. The number was so small for such a beautiful man it made him see red. Heath felt Nathan himself was slighted by his son's low bids, and that played a role, no doubt, in his sudden decision to type in a number of his own—a big number, the kind of number to give other bidders pause—and then hit enter.

Certainty surged through him. He could do this, handle the heat of Nathan's son and, with any luck, walk out of it with a child that was at least partially made up of the man he'd adored against all reason. Oh, Nathan…

Brilliant, charming, sadistic Nathan. How he'd loved the demon and the man, both.

He wouldn't make that same mistake with Adrien, though. He'd keep it clean. Unemotional. A transaction and nothing more. He'd promised himself after everything he'd endured that no omega would hold sway over him again. Not the way Nathan had. Losing him had hurt too much, wounded Heath too deeply.

Besides, no omega could ever hold a candle to Nathan, his beauty or his intellect, and definitely never his skill in the bedroom. There would be no risk to his heart.

Heath squeezed his cock and gazed again at the photo of the boy's asshole. It was a lovely swirl nestled between two sweet cheeks. Colored a gentle pinkish-brown, a bit darker than Nathan's had been, it was hairless and clearly untouched.

He stood, unbuckled his pants, and scrolled the page so he could see all four pictures of the boy at once. He tugged his thick cock free and groaned as he palmed it, squeezing as he massaged the length. Narrowing his eyes to slits, he stared at the screen and remembered Nathan in ecstasy. He jerked himself off fast and hard, hips pumping, as he gazed at his dead lover's son and imagined him as Nathan—on his knees, ass up, begging to be filled with babies and Heath's knot.

Grunting, he came, pulse after pulse of pleasure spurting out across the screen over the images of Adrien's face, body, ass, and hole. Shaken by the sharpness of his lust, Heath collapsed in his desk chair and glared at the screen as his bid was downgraded and the total number ticked up.

Wiping the screen clean, he leaned forward, cock still hard and sticking out from his open pants. Typing in a new set of numbers, he leaned back in satisfaction. Let someone try to take this boy from him. Just let them.

Taking hold of his cock again, he refreshed the page, making sure his bid stayed the highest. He'd have Nathan's grown son beneath him, and he'd breed the last remaining piece of the lover he'd lost, if it took ransoming his entire estate to do it.

ADRIEN GAPED AT the latest number associated with his auction. He couldn't believe the astronomical amounts that were still ever-so-slowly creeping higher. He'd be able to fund the rest of his studies easily, and even have more than enough to pay for the fee to be named a professor. There'd been a big jump on the third day of the auction for no reason he could discern, but once he'd allowed Ron to add breeding to his listing, the bids had gone gangbusters. He'd never imagined that breeding would be so valuable.

He just wished the idea of it didn't scare him so much.

Adrien knew very little about pregnancy outside of the elementary information he'd gleaned during his only human biology class at the beginning of his university career. It had been a class for omegas only. Segregated human biology classes were the norm for all but the most liberal of universities—curriculum divided between alphas, omegas, and betas, with extra information for alphas or betas on the medical school track.

It was considered a well-worn truth that omegas were better off knowing as little as possible about the experiences they would face, or else they might resist their heats. Alphas were to assume responsibility for guiding omegas through the trials and tribulations of their biology, and their classes were rumored to be more thorough. Most omegas learned about the joys and terrors of their biology from older omegas in their lives, but Adrien knew few of those, and none he was close enough with to ask questions regarding heat, pregnancy, and birth. It struck him as absurd that omegas were kept so in the dark and that the omega's physical, emotional, and spiritual state during the various stages of heat, pregnancy, and birth were more thoroughly covered in the classes for alphas.

He'd had so many questions during that human biology course. But he was new on campus, and lonely. He hadn't wanted to rock the boat or let anyone know how out of place he felt being at university after all the years of his father's religious teachings, so he'd kept most of his questions to himself.

Besides, at the time, his first season had seemed forever and a day away. He'd filled the time since that long ago class with deep studies into artistic techniques, fabric skills, and the science of materials, allowing himself to almost forget how little he knew about the ins and outs of human reproduction. But now the reality of his ignorance had all come down upon him at once.

What Adrien wouldn't do now to sit in on just one of those

alpha reproduction classes to better understand what he should expect to endure?

A knock came at his dorm room door. After quickly closing the auction tab, Adrien slid out of his chair and peered through the peephole to see who was waiting outside. He groaned when he recognized Lance's dark skin and fuzzy black hair. Dammit, he supposed there was no avoiding it any longer.

He opened the door and forced a smile. "Hey, Lance. How can I help you?"

Lance lifted a brow and pushed his way past Adrien into his dorm room. "Why have you been hiding in here for the last week? You passed your contribution to Professor Urgil's new article off to me, and you didn't even come sit in on the interview of the Hontu artist he brought in. You've been waiting to hear what that guy had to say all year!"

Adrien sat down on his mattress and motioned for Lance to take a seat in the chair by his desk. He'd completely forgotten about the interview with the Hontu artist. He'd been planning his questions for weeks: What does the blue dye made from Hontutua berries mean to your tribe? Is there a symbolism in its use? And other curiosities he'd hoped to satisfy in person since the Hontu were notoriously superstitious about written communications. Adrien cursed softly under his breath. How had he let that get past him? Shame. That's how.

Lance dropped into the chair and went on, "I thought you might be sick, but clearly you're not." He crossed his arms over his chest and tipped back so that the front legs of the chair came up off the floor recklessly. "Is this about the auction?"

Adrien's throat went dry. Of course it was about the auction! Whenever he even left his room to creep down the hall to use the communal showers and bathrooms, he felt the eyes of the other students all over him. They knew what he looked like naked now.

The size of his dick, the way his asshole crinkled, and the horrible vulnerability of his expression in his headshot. Everyone knew.

"Wow, look at you blush. It's like a full body thing. I bet even your thighs are red right now."

Adrien's glasses slipped down his nose as sweat popped up on his skin.

Lance huffed. "You're *embarrassed*? Dude, you should be proud. I don't know the last time an auction went this high. That's the only reason I even know about it." He clucked his tongue. "Some alpha in class was talking about how guys like him never stand a chance when the wealthy elite can outbid them by astronomical amounts. So I had to grab a look this uber-desirable omega, and hell, friend, it was you!"

"Yeah. Well." Adrien rubbed the back of his neck. "Me."

"Why are you so miserable?"

"It's all really…" Sordid? Frightening? "Strange. I don't know who's going to win me, and it's a little creepy, you know?"

"No. I don't know. What do you mean 'creepy'? It's just the way it is. How it's always been."

Adrien squirmed but held back his questions about why, and who invented the system, and who really benefited in the end.

Lance took pity on him and didn't push about his feelings, instead directing his questions to the auction itself. "So you really have no idea who the guy driving the price up is? *H. Battershell* is all it says. I bet it's a screen name. Some of these guys are private about their love for handling heats. Like it's something to be ashamed of." He rolled his eyes. "Whatever. Anyway, who is this guy?"

"No idea." Adrien waved off the question.

Lance's eyebrows drew low. "What's that mean? You don't care who he is?"

"I thought it wasn't supposed to matter. That it's 'the way it is' so..."

"So you're basically dying of curiosity, then."

"Of course I am! But they don't give you any information about the alpha until the bidding is over, and then it's only what he wants to share!"

Lance stared at him, cocked his head, and asked gently, "C'mon, Adrien. What's the real problem here? You should be happy. Excited. *Eager.*"

Adrien flopped back on his bed, exhaustion weighing him down like a pallet of bricks on his chest. "Sometimes I am, but other times I'm just plain scared. Don't tell me I shouldn't be."

"Okay, I won't." Lance sounded sympathetic. "I forget you didn't have an omega parent. Right? Just your alpha dad raised you, and he never took on another omega after you were born?"

Adrien shook his head.

"No close omega cousins or uncles?"

"No." Adrien sighed. "No one. We lived way out in the country, and the only time I saw other folks was when we went to church. There were other omegas there, obviously. But I've never even seen a pregnant one."

"Wow. I guess this would all be really overwhelming to you then. Especially since your father isn't here to help guide you through it all."

Adrien made a face at the thought of his father guiding him through this situation. Their church saw heats as the punishment omegas endured for daring to be like God and create something from nothing—to make life in their wombs. Adrien's father hadn't been as conservative as some, but he'd kept his lips tightly closed when it came to any discussion of sex. "Yeah. Overwhelming is a good word for it. And when I leave my dorm room, I feel like everyone's staring at me."

Lance cracked a smile and dropped the chair's front legs

down to the floor. "Because your hot little bod is racking up the dough!"

"Yeah, but they all know what my asshole looks like."

"Dude, it's an asshole." Lance laughed. "We all have one. Mine is darker than yours, like the rest of me, but it's not exactly different. Take heart."

Adrien refrained from pointing out that a dozen alphas were competing at astronomical prices for access to *his* asshole, so it must be pretty special, even if neither of them could see a reason why.

"I'm nervous," Adrien said. "I don't know who this guy is, or what he looks like, or how old he is, or if he's rough or sweet or kind?"

"There are protections in place. A vetting process," Lance explained. "The alphas bidding for access to you aren't all gorgeous, but none of them are going to hurt you, either." Lance smirked. "Not unless you're selling that, too. Some omegas do."

"No!" Adrien's eyes bugged.

"I know, I know." Lance laughed again and put out a calming hand. "I saw your listing."

"Alphas won't try to convince me to do that during my heat, will they?" Adrien asked, remembering how Ron had said that alphas would sometimes try to convince omegas in the throes of heat to add on breeding at a reduced rate.

"No. There are rules about that. Breeding can be added if an omega consents"—Lance shifted uncomfortably as if even he doubted consent mid-heat—"but pain and all of that has to be negotiated up front." He leaned forward and rested his elbows on his knees. "I admit I was surprised to see breeding since I know you're in so deep with the Hontu project. You've been so dedicated to seeing it through. But it was a good choice financially, obviously."

"How do you know so much about how it all works?"

"My father's omegas and I talk. They knew I wouldn't get the information I needed in that stupid class they make us take. Traditionally, it falls to the omega parent to pass this information on, or, if you don't have an omega parent, to the omega friends of the family or your father's new omegas"

"Yeah, I don't..." Adrien lifted his hands helplessly.

"I know. But...damn, friend. How is it that you're so alone in the world?" Lance asked, a hint of pity flavoring his words. "Even in that little community, I'd have thought the omegas would take you under their wing."

"Just bad luck, I guess," Adrien said, and sighed.

"Tell me more. What was your father like?"

"He was deeply religious."

"Oh? That's unusual in this day and age. A throwback?"

"Yeah. It was a very small community. There weren't a lot of omegas for alphas to choose from, though, so my father had to buy a heat to have me. He saved a long time to afford a good one."

"Wasn't that looked down on?"

"Necessity breeds generosity. They understood his predicament."

"What do you think of all that? Religion and church?"

Adrien sighed and rubbed his hands through his hair. "I guess some of his ideas stuck with me and some didn't."

"I suppose that explains why you're so shy about your body," Lance teased. "Always wearing that ridiculous robe into the dorm showers, like someone's gonna ogle your chest if you just wrap a towel around your ass."

"My father taught me modesty was important."

"Your father had ideas that aren't going to serve you well," Lance said, gently. "Being an omega? It involves a lot of nakedness, and, frankly, giving in to your inner slut."

"What if I don't have an inner slut?"

"Oh, you do." Lance laughed again.

Adrien let his head fall back, and he examined his dorm room ceiling for a few quiet moments, grateful for Lance's friendship and feeling stupid for avoiding him now. "Will you choose breeding?" Adrien asked.

"Definitely. It's a done deal. My contract is signed and sealed, you know. A year and a half from now, I'll go meet up with my father's friend John and get stuffed with his dick, *and* his kid, if all goes to plan." Somehow, Lance managed to make it sound like he thought that was dreamy.

"Sexy."

"You know it." Lance grinned. "C'mon, loosen up. Once you're in heat, you won't care what the guy looks like, or how old he is, so long as he knots you and makes you cum. That's the way it works. My father's omegas promised me that much."

Adrien shivered. "I guess I want more than that."

Lance chuckled. "Go on. Say it."

"I want someone to love me."

"Of course you do," he said, kindly. "We all want that. And with you being without any family at all, you must want that even more. But here's the thing, Adrien, you can have that someday, but probably not now. Unfortunately, it's time for your first season, and you've been so introverted—"

"Dedicated to my studies!"

"Whatever. Fine, dedicated to your studies. What I'm saying is that you've never put yourself out there. You've never looked for anyone to satisfy that need for you—which makes sense now that I know more about where you came from. In those religious communities, alphas do all the flirting and courting, don't they?"

"Yes."

"Right. And so, right now, you're out in the real world, where omegas are the ones who are supposed to convince alphas they're worth taking on. So, yeah. At this point, you're going to have to take whoever wins you for this heat." He said it as compassionately as possible, but Adrien couldn't help but hear the echo of his father's urging throughout his life: *Make friends, Adrien, go to church more often, smile at the alphas there! One day you'll need them to want you, boy, and you'll want them to love you.*

But he'd always been too shy.

Lance kept talking, "But, hey, it's not the end of the world. See this as an adventure and an opportunity. Besides, you never know, this could actually lead to you finding *the one*. Mr. H. Battershell could be your dream man."

"You're such a romantic."

"I can't help it. It's just the way I'm made." Lance stood and shoved his hands in his pockets. "Please, Adrien. Come to class tomorrow and get back to our research. You've only got a few weeks before the heat auction is over, and then you'll be absent. I know you'll want to learn all that you can about that Hontu dye. And, yeah, if people are staring it's because they're jealous at what a rich young man you're about to be."

Adrien nodded and tried to make his voice sound like Lance's cheering up had worked. "You're right."

Lance winked. "And maybe they're staring just a little because your asshole is super-duper hot."

Adrien rolled his eyes. Still, he couldn't help but smile. "Thanks. I guess."

"Anytime."

# Chapter Four

ONE WEEK LATER, the auction closed with Adrien's bids at a near-record high, coming in second only behind a young man twenty-two years prior—the first to ever offer breeding in his auction price.

The winner of Adrien's heat was, of course, H. Battershell. Adrien had already used the Internet and the university library's resources to try to find any information about H. Battershell, but there was nothing. Clearly, he was using an alias. Aside from H. Battershell having bid on some young men's heats over ten years prior, records showed he hadn't been involved in auctions for quite some time.

When he asked Ron Finch about details on Battershell, he only got a bunch of blather about how the man was wealthy, and private, and that Adrien should be honored that he'd taken an interest in him at all.

"So I don't even get to know his name in advance?"

"He's been explicit with his instructions. He will give you all the information you need about him in person."

Adrien struggled to pull in a breath. It felt like bands had tightened around his torso at Mr. Finch's words. "Okay," he managed to say.

Mr. Finch tutted at him, like he was a naughty little boy for asking questions and then he gave Adrien the pills that were supposed to jumpstart his heat. "When the prickling begins, you'll know it's working." He passed on a note with an address and a date stamped on it. "You'll meet him there in four days. Arrive before noon. He wants the heat to already be kicking in when you get there, so be sure to start the pills immediately."

"Is that normal?" He'd hoped to have some time with the alpha beforehand.

Mr. Finch shrugged. "Some men like to spend a few days together pre-heat to get to know each other. Others want to leap right into the main event. He's a main event kind of guy. You have transportation, don't you?"

"Yes. I have a car."

"Excellent. You can drive yourself, unless your heat feels too far gone, and then we'll arrange for a driver. That address is up in the mountains. Be sure to map out how to get there in advance. There isn't a lot of cell service where you're headed."

Adrien swallowed hard. He'd be alone in the woods without cell service with a man he knew nothing about, vulnerable, and begging. Everything felt cold and hot at once. "Are there any pictures of him or…?"

"No. He'll meet you at that address. Remember, the money is held in escrow by the university until the heat and breeding are accomplished. Then, regardless of whether or not a pregnancy takes, they'll pass it on into your account."

Adrien nodded. "I see. Thank you."

"I'm proud of you, kid. Not everyone can bring in numbers like that. I have to admit you surprised me." Ron smirked and waved Adrien out the door. "Good luck to you."

Good luck to him? That was all? He was on his own now? Adrien's gut danced anxiously as he considered the next four days. He shook a pill out of the bottle and tossed it into his mouth as he walked back to his dorm. He knew it was all in his head, but as soon as he swallowed the pill, he started to feel a little warm.

He wiped at his sweaty forehead and hoped he wouldn't lose his nerve. It wasn't like he had a choice anyway. There was no chance to back out now.

THE HOUSE WAS a cabin in the woods. Small for a man with so much money to burn, but what did Adrien really know about that? Maybe H. Battershell liked to keep things simple despite his immense wealth. Adrien's father would have admired that.

The cabin was definitely isolated. If Adrien got spooked and wanted to run, he wouldn't get very far on foot. Perhaps that was why Battershell had chosen it. He slid his hand over the steering wheel to reassure himself that at least he had his car.

Putting it in park, he turned off the engine and straightened his glasses. In the trunk, he had his luggage. Enough clothes for a week of heat and a few days of recovery time, as well as the usual toiletries one needed on a trip away from home. His insides tangled like a burning, writhing, seething pile of snakes, making him squirm. He'd sported an erection and endured a slick, wet asshole since before he'd even left the dorm that morning. The evidence that his heat was coming on strong was indisputable, but he wasn't suffering from the mindless need to rut that he'd heard so much about. He supposed that was still ahead of him.

Adrien opened the car door and stretched. His asshole released another rush of slick, and he trembled. Not knowing how long he had before he lost reason and sanity in the primal irrationality of heat, he hoped he was able to meet Battershell and feel safe before that happened. Right now, everything about his current situation left him weak-kneed and nauseous with nerves.

The door to the cabin opened, and a darkly bearded man

came onto the porch, where he stood and stared hungrily at Adrien. His eyes appeared gray beneath thick brows, and he was taller than Adrien by at least four inches. His body was well-honed, with strong thighs and muscular arms. He stood barefoot and wore dark jeans and a tight black T-shirt that gripped his pecs and biceps. Not exactly the vision of a man of extraordinary means, but Adrien didn't know what he'd been expecting when he'd input the address into his GPS that morning. A mansion and a suit, perhaps? Servants holding the door of his car open and showing him into a glittering, mammoth home? Possibly.

Not this small cabin for sure.

"My name's Heath," the man said, and his voice was a low rumble that wrapped around Adrien and gripped him by the balls. "But you'll call me 'sir' until I say otherwise."

Adrien swallowed the sudden lump of fear in his throat. "Yes, okay."

"Yes, okay, what?"

"Yes, okay, sir?"

"That's right, Adrien."

It didn't go unnoticed that Heath had assumed full permission to use Adrien's name, but he didn't think it was wise to bring up the double standard. Not when his anus was starting to burn and his cock was throbbing in his own soft jeans. He moaned as Heath stepped toward him, walking down the short set of stairs between the cabin's porch and the pine-needle-strewn ground.

Heath stopped in front of him, raised a thick, dark brow and said, "Your profile pictures didn't show glasses."

Adrien touched the stems and said, "I can take them off, sir."

Heath nodded and put out his hand. Adrien removed his glasses, the world around him immediately going fuzzy and less defined. He put the glasses in Heath's hand, feeling even more vulnerable without being able to make out the crisp lines of Heath's face.

"Strip," Heath ordered. "You won't need your clothes from this point forward." He motioned toward the luggage in the back seat of Adrien's car. "Or any of those other things, either. I paid for your heat and for breeding you. That means these next few days, or however long it takes for your heat to pass, are mine to command."

Adrien squinted, trying to make out if Heath was joking. He wasn't sure if that was how it worked, actually. He'd never asked anyone who'd been through a heat what was expected. He wished he'd asked Lance more about it. Even though he'd never had his own first heat, he seemed to know a lot about it. Adrien didn't move for a long moment, considering Heath's words. But Heath stared at him so confidently, with so much intensity, that he could make it out even with his blurred vision, and he eventually found himself unbuttoning his shirt with shaking fingers.

"That's good," Heath said as Adrien slipped his shirt from his shoulders and let it flutter to the ground. "Kick off your shoes. Good. The pants now. Everything."

Adrien glanced around the clearing in front of the house, uncertain of being naked outside. Due to his religious upbringing and natural shyness, he'd never been one for public displays of his body, even preferring to wear a swim shirt when at the pool. But there was no one in these deep, shadowy, silent woods but him and Heath. He took in the swaying and creaking of the trees around him, the gray depth of the shadows stretching into the dark forest, and felt the cool breeze flowing over his now-exposed skin. His nipples peaked, and he shuddered as he undid his jeans quickly and shoved them down.

Heath crossed his arms over his chest, glasses still clutched in one hand, when Adrien stood up straight after removing his socks. His gaze crawled over Adrien's body, head to toe, in a slow, assessing way. "Fold the clothes. Put them and your glasses back in the car for safe keeping."

Adrien did as he was told, slick sliding down his legs, and his hands trembling madly.

"Turn around," Heath said, when he was done.

Trembling, Adrien complied. With his back to Heath, he faced the long, twisted driveway through the forest. He peered down it wondering what he'd sold, exactly, when he agreed to do the online auction. His dignity? His soul?

"Bend over. Spread your cheeks. I want to see what I paid for."

Adrien's throat clicked as he swallowed, and some part of him thought of protesting. But his cock ached against his stomach, pre-cum welling up and slipping down the sides, and his asshole leaked lubricating slick relentlessly, leaving his thighs a wet mess. His hole clenched and released with restless need. Taking a deep breath, he did as he was ordered.

A breeze fluttered over his hot, wet anus, and he moaned at the touch of nature on his most private place. He squeezed his eyes closed and waited, and then he felt a dam break inside. Lust flooded him. He fought it for a moment, fear and disorientation mounting.

"Shh, steady," Heath whispered.

Adrien moaned and arched into the brush of Heath's hand down his back, around his buttocks.

"I've got you now." With no hesitation, Heath's solid, firm fingers invaded his aching hole. He moaned as two of them slipped in deep, found his heat-swollen prostate, and massaged it while Adrien struggled for balance. He pushed his hands into his thighs and groaned as another obliterating wave of lust swallowed him up.

Just as Adrien's knees started to give out, lost to uncompromising need and humping back against Heath's intruding digits, Heath yanked his fingers free. "Stand up," he ordered. "Turn around to face me."

Panting like a slut, he was dizzy and begging for—something. He didn't know what. An end, a start? A climax? He was wild with it now and pleading sounds spilled out of his mouth. Nothing mattered but being touched and reaching satisfaction. It was exactly as Lance had warned him.

Adrien turned. His entire body jittered with the rising heat, and he gave in to the strange eroticism of this man commanding him in such an intimate way.

"Please," Adrien whispered. "Hurry. I want, I need, please."

Heath stepped back from Adrien, provoking a cry, and gave him another long once-over before undoing his own jeans and shoving them down to bring out his enormous cock. Adrien's breath stuttered as he took in the vast width and length, and his asshole ran with slick, preparing itself for the mammoth intrusion. He'd always known that alpha cocks were larger than omegas' or betas'; they'd covered that even in omega sex education classes in school. He'd seen plenty of porn in his life, too, but he'd never imagined a cock could be the size of Heath's.

Nor did he know it would smell so good. His mouth watered and he wanted to taste the wet tip of the enormous thing.

"Get on your knees," Heath said, stroking his hand over his tool, milking a bead of pre-cum from the slit.

Adrien hesitated for a moment, but then a massive rush of slick flooded his thighs and a slam of heat rolled over his body. Lust had him in its grip, and he fell to his knees, crying out with want. The full expression of heat was on him and rational thought evaporated into sensation and desire. His cock bobbed against his stomach, the line of fur between his belly button and pubic mound teasing and scratching maddeningly.

"Very good," Heath said, but there was no smile in his eyes. No glimmer of amusement or affection. Only authority and lust. Perhaps a touch of concern, though Adrien's heat-addled mind couldn't be sure.

His asshole ached and burned, an itch that washed over his entire body and then exploded against his skin. He threw his head back and shouted, his anus convulsing desperately. The breeze over him was a maddening caress, and the emptiness of his body was so consuming that he no longer felt human.

He was raw, needful, aching flesh from head to toe—craving only cock, and cum, and orgasm, and needing only an alpha's knot. He whimpered, dazed and lost. He thrust his ass in the air, hands on the ground, knees in the dirt.

"That's right," Heath said with a crooked smirk. "This is heat. How do you like it so far?"

Adrien moaned and shifted from knee to knee, his cock a tempting rod of flesh that he wanted to grip and jerk. But some part of him knew better than to touch himself without permission in front of an alpha. So he groveled there, prickling with need, and gazed up at Heath with desperation sliding all over his face.

"Beautiful," Heath muttered. "So much like…"

But he didn't finish that sentence. Instead, his eyes, which had softened when presented with Adrien's display of needy vulnerability, hardened again. "Crawl to me. Mouth open, tongue out."

Adrien crawled, his aching hard cock swinging as he did, and his slick asshole screaming for cock. He stuck his tongue out as far as he could and opened his mouth wide as he finally reached the space at Heath's bare feet. He glimpsed tufts of dark hair on the joint of each of Heath's toes, and then gasped. He *needed* to bend and kiss them. *Wanted* to.

He did just that.

Heath chuckled above him. "All the right instincts," he said, and then tugged Adrien up by the hair. "Lick my balls." He brought Adrien's face between his legs, shoving his nose against his groin.

As Adrien obeyed, his tongue bathing Heath's soft, hairy sac and mouthing his big, round, alpha-sized testicles, Heath gripped his hair tightly, holding him in place. With his other hand, he stroked Adrien's neck and shoulders soothingly, his breath coming in harsh shudders. A soft groan escaped as Adrien became more dedicated to his job.

Leaning over Adrien's back, while Adrien continued to work, Heath slipped his fingers down Adrien's back. Releasing Heath's sac from his mouth, Adrien buried his nose in Heath's scratchy pubes, breathing in the rough, musky scent of an aroused alpha. He couldn't get enough of it, sucking in breath after breath.

"Stand up." Heath hauled Adrien to his feet, cradling him close so that his mouth rested against the thrumming pulse of Heath's neck. He put out his tongue and tasted it. Clenching Adrien to him with one arm, Heath slid his hand down to touch Adrien's gaping, wet hole. He plunged three fingers in roughly. Adrien let loose a begging sound against Heath's throat. The pressure on his heat-enlarged prostate made him feel like he was going to burst out of his skin with desire. He groaned and grunted, fucking back against Heath's hand, the small rocks in the dirt of the clearing digging into his feet. He clutched Heath's strong back and whimpered madly, finally mouthing his neck and sucking in sheer desperation.

"What a sweet little slut you're turning out to be," Heath murmured, still fucking three thick fingers into Adrien's slick, wet hole.

Adrien shook and convulsed, his asshole tightening around Heath's fingers. Every filthy word of praise from Heath was aural bliss to Adrien, and he shivered with pleasure at every syllable.

"That's it," Heath said, shoving Adrien down to his knees again. Guiding his thick dickhead into Adrien's panting, open mouth, he ordered, "Suck me."

Adrien greedily complied, the taste of Heath's musky jizz enflaming him even more. He wanted to throw himself onto the dirt, lift his ass up again, and beg to be mounted. But with his mouth stuffed full of cock, he was pinned in place. His hands gripped Heath's jean-clad thighs as he fought to breathe around the thickness. He burned and yearned, nerves screaming *more*, and *please*, and *knot me*. His lungs screamed for oxygen.

Heath sounded like he was smiling when he said, "Yes, Adrien. Yes. You were made to squeeze my knot. A perfect fuckhole."

Adrien whimpered and groaned his agreement as he sucked harder on the head of Heath's fat cock. It was all he could fit in his mouth, and even so, the stretched edges of his lips burned as he attempted more.

"Ready and eager. Just like I knew you would be. Such a good omega slut."

The crass words combined with more praise set Adrien off. He released Heath's cock, holding it in his hand instead, as he cried out. Then he tossed his head back, gritting his teeth together, and rode the wave of burning lust that nearly turned him inside out.

"Come for me," Heath commanded, gripping Adrien's hair and shoving Adrien's face against his flexing thigh. "Get your cock in your hand and make yourself come."

Adrien hastened to obey. His entire body was strung so tight he felt on the verge of dying—his pulse banging, his chest tight, the tension of his body as he rode the intense lust was too much.

He couldn't survive this. Not unless he got a knot in his ass to satisfy his craving. His cock was an iron-hot rod in his hand, and he worked it fast.

"Take your pleasure. It's what your body's for."

Heath tugged his hair brutally with one hand and gently stroked his back with the other. Adrien scrambled at the jeans covering Heath's thighs, holding on as the keen feeling crested, and then he screamed, coming hard. With each powerful burst, he left thick ropes of musky jizz on the ground.

Heath slipped his fingers free from Adrien's hair, setting off a shockwave of need that left him dizzy. He gripped Heath harder to make sure he didn't fall over. His cum coated several of Heath's toes and soaked into the brown dirt under Heath's feet. He stared at it, the heat and lust that had driven him barely easing.

"Lick it up," Heath said calmly. "From my feet. Clean my toes."

Sweaty and tired, but still driven to want more, Adrien bent and licked his cum from Heath's toes, his balls tingling with renewing arousal. How? He'd just come. Didn't he get any kind of break from this?

Heath smoothed a hand through Adrien's hair calmingly. "Good boy."

Adrien warmed all over at the praise and whimpered, mouthing at Heath's crotch. His cock hardened again, and he moaned.

"Yes. You're an unexpectedly good boy. Let's get you inside."

# Chapter Five

HEATH WAS ALREADY pleased with his decision to participate in the auction. Aside from Adrien's connection to Nathan, the boy himself was delicious and fresh, so very new to sensation that it was a delight watching him succumb to the heat.

Shaking all over and bleary-eyed with unquenchable lust, despite his recent orgasm, Adrien had to be nearly carried up the stairs and into the cabin. Heath laughed under his breath as Adrien fell to his knees again the moment they were over the threshold in his hurry to get Heath's cock and balls back into his mouth.

Hungrily, he jerked Heath's pants down his hips so he could rub his face all over Heath's crotch.

Heath had planned to take the boy to the cabin's one bedroom and fuck him properly there on the bed for the first time, but his own control was slipping fast. He was ready for the wet, slick heat of Adrien's body, and even if he ended up regretting knotting the boy for the first time on the entryway floor, he didn't care right now.

"Get into position," Heath growled, shoving Adrien away from his balls.

Adrien fell to the floor, ass up, legs spread. He shook all over, his naked body trembling and his pale skin marked red from the roughness of Heath's hands as he'd carried him in. "Please, please," he whispered, completely out of his mind now. Just the way Heath liked it best with omegas he didn't know. Though he preferred the hint of recognition he'd always seen behind the all-consuming lust in Nathan's brilliant eyes.

Heath shoved his jeans down and off, and ripped his T-shirt over his head and tossed it across the room before kneeling naked behind Adrien. He massaged Adrien's glistening asshole with his thumbs and then pressed the head of his cock against the opening. Adrien's body broke out into sweat, and the scent pummeled Heath's self-control. It was hard to hold back when the boy—who looked so much like Nathan, and even moved like him, too—was writhing in needful desire on the floor, hitching his ass back trying to get Heath inside. It was easy to almost let himself *feel something*. To let his emotions slip back in time.

But no…

"You're a hungry little fucksleeve," Heath said, slapping Adrien's backside and grinning when he jumped. But then he relented, whispering, "Relax. I'll take care of you."

Because he wasn't a monster. This was Adrien's first time—ever—and he deserved an alpha who'd see to his pleasure and his needs. All omegas deserved that, even if they couldn't, in the scheme of life, be trusted to be gentle with an alpha's heart.

Heath pushed his cock against Adrien's hole harder and bit his own lip to stifle a moan as the slick ring opened around him. Adrien shouted, his body going rigid and his rim stretching thin around the girth of Heath's cockhead.

"Breathe," Heath murmured. "Bear down. That's a good boy."

Adrien quivered and followed instructions, his back muscles jumping as he struggled to accept the invasion of Heath's cock. Heath made a soothing noise, and gave more words of praise when Adrien's asshole opened with a sudden release of tension, sucking Heath halfway in.

Adrien vibrated on Heath's cock, his head tossed back, his muscles straining and tense, and his hole gripping the wide shaft of Heath's dick firmly. Belatedly, Heath wished he'd done this with Adrien lying down faceup, so he could better see the boy's face and gauge his pain level from his eyes, but the deed was done. He rubbed Adrien's lower back gently, shushing him and quieting the panic from his body.

"You feel wonderful," he whispered.

"Thank you, sir," Adrien replied.

A softness started in his heart, like a bruise. He tried to harden against it, but Adrien's ass was so hot inside, so silky and tight. It left him lightheaded and hopeful. He squeezed his eyes shut to fight the powerful connection between an alpha and omega before it engaged his emotions against his will.

Grunting, he gripped Adrien's hips, determined to master himself. He decided he was glad Adrien was facedown to obscure his resemblance to Nathan lest his too tender heart betray his mind. "Open up, little one. It only gets better from here."

*Little one*? Damn his tongue. Damn his tenderness. Most of all, damn the cursed softness in him that had led him to fall for Nathan to begin with, the same unwanted kindness that also led him to continually dig his asshole nephew out of too many messes. This was the main reason he'd stopped taking on omegas' heats years ago, because he couldn't help but surrender to a certain tenderness for them. His heart was always overripe, like fruit bruised by a rough grip. It was their fault, wasn't it? He couldn't help but respond to an alluring omega submitting to his cock.

Even when they didn't yield *their* heart or mind at all.

No, Nathan had always had all the emotional control.

Heath struggled to harden himself again.

Adrien bowed his head and convulsed twice before ceding to

Heath's command. His muscles relaxed, and his body slipped down to the floor. Heath hissed gently, and that damned tenderness returned so that his chest ached with unearned affection. He closed his eyes and told himself that these feelings were only the start of a heat crush.

Many considered heat crushes healthy. Good. More likely to result in a pregnancy. Not to mention pleasurable. The swoop and rush of an infatuation always was enjoyable, after all. Heath shoved his cock deeper and made up his mind to appreciate his experience with Nathan's son. It was okay to feel this sympathy for his young, confused omega, because no doubt the feeling would pass along with the boy's lust when the week was done. A heat crush was fine. He wouldn't fall in love.

Gripping Adrien's hips, Heath slid all the way in, throwing his head back and groaning when his balls pressed against Adrien's flesh and the boy's channel spasmed around him. Slick rushed out around his cock, coating his balls and making his thighs damp.

Adrien flushed hard, his entire back, the back of his neck, and the tips of his ears going pink, and Heath smiled. The unforgiving lust of his first season was on the boy fully now.

He slid out slightly, pushed back in, and groaned as Adrien's heat-swollen prostate massaged the underside of his cock. Adrien shuddered all over, and when Heath thrust again, nailing that gland hard, the boy lost control. His cock spurted all over the floor, his body flailed desperately as he hit an unexpected height of pleasure, and he cried out in shock. Heath gripped his hips even more firmly and fucked him hard and fast, greedily watching for every moment of pleasure.

Heath's inner alpha loved seeing Adrien reduced to a slick-gushing, asshole-gaping, mouth-drooling, cum-greedy omega in heat, all other trace of his humanity and personality stripped away in his desperate need for Heath's knot. But the sympathetic man in him wanted Adrien to enjoy it, too. To love being fucked and filled. To open himself to the sexual delights on offer to him as an omega, the pleasures he could enjoy for the rest of his life.

Heath dug his fingers in harder, holding onto Adrien's hips as the boy came yet again. The scent of his jizz rose to Heath's sensitive nose. He thrust firmly as Adrien's cries rose and fell, crescendos of pleasure again and again. Adrien suddenly went still, taking Heath's thrusts with a tension that Heath recognized as the ultimate heat orgasm rising. The climactic gratification that would rip Adrien's soul open and leave him in a state of shock while Heath knotted him.

Sure enough, Adrien screamed—the terror of pleasure sounding every bit as scary as any other overwhelming thing—and then his whole body seized. His asshole spasmed around Heath in rhythm with his cries and convulsions, his body erupted in goosebumps, and his heartbeat thrummed visibly in his temples and throat.

Heath shoved in deep and held on tight as his own orgasm throttled him. He rode it out, spurting into Adrien's womb and biting his lip to keep from screaming in pleasure. He held still as the intense initial phase of his orgasm passed. Then the second phase began. He groaned, shifting as his cock expanded, the base ballooning with blood, knotting him into Adrien's asshole, holding them together, and trapping them in place.

Adrien crumpled to the hard floor in a glassy-eyed daze, his cock spurting small amounts of cum with each twitch of his body. Heath collapsed onto his back, his cock similarly sending out brief jets of semen in response to Adrien's hole convulsively gripping his substantial and still-growing knot.

"Oh my God," Adrien finally whispered, when Heath was fully enlarged inside him. The tight-fitting channel around his knot pulsed with Adrien's heartbeat. Heath wrapped his arms around Adrien's smaller body and clung to him like a raft as the knotting phase persisted.

The pleasure came in waves, a fast tide of orgasms that left his legs numb and his balls aching. Heath chuckled into Adrien's sweat-damp hair. It was only the first knot of the heat; what pleasure was still ahead for them. Adrien lay beneath him, still and quiet, his legs twitching from time to time and his cock sending out a small gush occasionally. His breath came in shallow, panicked gasps, and his body felt tight as a spring in Heath's arms.

Dragging himself out of his knotting-stupor, Heath said, "Just breathe. This lasts a long time. Enjoy it."

"How?" Adrien whispered.

"Isn't my knot pressing your prostate?"

"Yes, sir," Adrien agreed.

"Doesn't it feel good?"

"It does...but, I'm scared, sir."

"Am I hurting you?"

"I'm..."Adrien cleared his throat and then gasped as a bolt of pleasure seemed to distract him for a moment. "I feel trapped," he finally said. "It scares me that I'm stuck here."

Heath kissed the back of the boy's neck, cuddling him to try to calm him down. "This is just the start, little one. When it's all said and done, I'll knot you like this upward of fifteen times. Trust me. You're safe. Relax and enjoy this connection with the father of your child."

Adrien shivered against him. "You're so sure I'll fall pregnant?"

"I demand it." The floor dug into his knees and hips, and he noticed that Adrien's face was a bit smashed against the floorboards in their current position. He carefully slipped his arms under Adrien again and rolled them so that Adrien's head rested on Heath's forearm and not the hard floor.

The movement pushed his knot into Adrien's prostate, though, and the boy cried out as he came again. His ass milking Heath's knot made him groan and bite down on the tendon between Adrien's shoulder and neck as he shot more cum into the boy's womb.

When the new shock had passed, Adrien relaxed in his arms. His body was warm and fit against Heath's perfectly. He fought the urge to cuddle him closer, to kiss the nape of his neck, and to pretend he was Nathan.

Adrien asked, uncertainly, "Sir? Are we allowed to be friends? Or do we just…fuck?"

Heath bit down a chuckle. There went the idea of pretending he was Nathan. He sounded far too innocent and confused for that. Nathan would never have called him 'sir' in all seriousness. What a darling omega he had hold of, so young and sweet. Though not quite trusting. He nuzzled the back of Adrien's neck. He sighed when he realized what he'd done. *Just a heat crush. Make it a transaction.* "As the heat comes on harder, you'll find there are fewer lulls between the intense periods of need—"

"You mean it gets more intense than this?" Adrien gasped.

Good God, who had failed to teach this boy the basics? Heath blinked back his surprise, but then ran a calming hand over Adrien's flanks and said as matter-of-factly as possible, "It does. Eventually it's *all* this—for a day or so. And you don't know up from down, or if you're hungry or thirsty. All you are is sensation and pleasure and orgasm."

"Fuck," Adrien hissed. "I don't know if I'll survive it. Uh, sir."

"I've never known an omega to die from it yet," Heath said, kissing the back of Adrien's neck again. "Not if their alpha makes sure they stay hydrated."

Adrien licked his lips. "I am a little thirsty. Sir. Sorry, I meant to say sir."

"Once my knot goes down, I'll get you food and water, and see you safely to the bed. You don't have to call me sir."

"I don't?"

"No." Heath didn't find it nearly as appealing without the sneer and smirk Nathan had given it. It just made him feel sad, like Adrien wasn't connecting to him the way he should—especially for his first season.

"What should I call you then?"

"You can call me Heath."

"Heath…" Adrien sighed and said it again. "I like that."

Heath said nothing, unwilling to admit even to himself that Adrien's words pleased him.

"Is it common to end up on the floor like this?" Adrien asked after a few long minutes.

Heath shrugged. "Alphas have different ways of doing things."

The shrug set off another spasm in Adrien. He hunched back on Heath's cock, clenching and whimpering. "This is so embarrassing," he said once he finally stopped coming again.

"Is it?" Heath pondered the thought. He supposed it must be odd to be so vulnerable and raw, pinned like a bug on a stranger's cock.

"I can't stop coming. And I don't…I don't even know you."

He'd been right then. That's what it was all about. "You know that I'm an alpha and you're an omega. We come together like this and create life. There's little else to it."

Adrien shivered and said nothing. He relaxed in Heath's arms after a bit, and they lay on the hard floor together waiting. Adrien drowsed and Heath took the time to really study his profile. His long, straight nose was handsome, and so like Nathan's. His blond lashes lay on his cheek, a brighter gold than Nathan's had been. That was one of the few differences. Adrien's build was so like his omega father's had been that, if Heath closed his eyes, he could almost fool his heart into believing he held Nathan in his arms.

Except for the scent. Which was entirely different but not at all repellent. Adrien's scent was...delicious even. In its own way. A fruity sort of musk combined with his own spunk and the sweetness of Adrien's slick.

Eventually, his knot began to recede, and when it was completely gone, he tugged out of Adrien's body, waking the boy with the odd sensation of a giant cock leaving his gaping ass.

Adrien hissed and doubled over.

"Cramps," Heath explained. "I stretched your insides with the knot. It's hard for your body to adjust. Just breathe through it."

Then he rose and went into the bedroom, leaving Adrien on the floor, breath hitching with the cramping pain. He returned and knelt by Adrien's side and slid a thick rubber plug into him.

Adrien groaned and twitched. "What's...?"

"To hold you open so my entry is easier next time, and to keep my semen inside you to increase the chances of pregnancy. Also to reduce cramping."

Adrien trembled on the floor for a few seconds, but when Heath stood and reached down to help Adrien up, his hand gripped Heath's solidly.

On his feet again, Adrien looked healthy enough, but a little thin. His skin was taut over his muscles, showing off every tendon and bulge. Heath had heard the boy's aesthetic called 'stringy,' but he ideally preferred a man with a little more flesh under his skin. Still, something about Adrien's body and form called to Heath on a primal level—he ached to keep the boy safe, to feed him delicious foods and plump him up, and to fill him with his cock.

And most of all to see him birth Heath's children.

What had started as a desire to join his genes with Nathan's was morphing, even after only this first fuck, to include a desire to see what Adrien himself might offer as a man, omega, and father. Heath squeezed his eyes shut. Ridiculous heat crush! He'd fight against it, but there was only so much he could do. Biology was a strict commander until the rush of heat was over.

Heath shook his head softly to dislodge unwarranted, heat-induced romantic thoughts before leading Adrien through to the bedroom. He flipped on the lamp by the bed, keeping the room dim, so that Adrien wouldn't be distracted from the otherworldly heat-dream that often overtook omegas and helped them relax when the lust gripped them hard.

"Climb in," he said, holding up the covers and gesturing toward the fresh sheets on the mattress. He'd put them on himself in preparation for their time together. According to the stories of old, it was the little things between alphas and omegas, like clean sheets and preparing food and water, which promoted an emotional attachment and thus improved the receptivity of an omega's womb. Scientifically, he knew that an omega could still be impregnated, emotional attachment or not, and originally he'd been determined to resist any such connection. But he also knew culture and biology both worked together to the benefit of a conceived child, and that included engaging the caring, protective, even possessive instinct of the alpha.

Yes, he was aware of all of this intellectually, but he was still surprised to find himself following instinct in such a blind way.

Adrien blinked toward the dim shadows and then obeyed Heath, sliding between the covers with a whimpering sigh. The scent of their sweat and cum transferred from Adrien's body to the bed, and it rose from the sheets as Heath fluffed them. His cock twitched, interest reignited, and he hoped Adrien's next wave of lust hit soon.

In the meantime, though, food and water were a must.

Leaving Adrien stunned and exhausted in bed, he went to the small kitchen, donned an apron, and checked the soup on the stove. It was a hearty meat stew with chunky vegetables that his grandfather had always prepared for his omegas during breeding, and Heath had twelve uncles, so it must provide sufficient nourishment. His own father had stuck to only one omega, married him, endured years of unhappy marriage, and had only two sons, but that had been their choice.

After filling a bowl, he brought it in to Adrien, along with a giant tumbler of water. Climbing carefully onto the bed next to his wide-eyed young purchase, he ordered him to sit up and eat.

Adrien's hands shook enough that the stew slopped a bit, and so, frowning, Heath took over. He fed him spoonful after spoonful, staring at his lips glistening with the greasy stew and listening for his soft sounds of satisfaction.

"This is good, Heath," Adrien murmured.

Heath said nothing in reply. He grew harder, his apron tenting, as he watched Adrien's throat bob with each swallow, and he imagined the heat of the boy's plump lips against his skin and the spasm of his throat around his cock.

When he was through and the bowl put away, Adrien sipped water greedily, a sheen of nervous, yearning energy glimmering over him. Heath sat beside him, staring at him, marking all the ways he was like Nathan and all the ways he was different. Same mouth, same forehead and chin, but the color of his hair was more golden than wheat, and the color of his eyes were brown rather than the pure, crystal blue of Nathan's.

The similarities were comforting, like coming home to a

warm blanket and comfortable bed after traveling far into the harsh world. But the differences were arousing. A newness that tingled in his balls and made him want to fuck Adrien again and knot him for hours. He hadn't expected that.

"Am I allowed to talk?" Adrien whispered, glancing anxiously toward Heath. "Or is this just a thing where we fuck and you knock me up, and once I give birth we go about our lives like we never met?"

"You can talk," Heath said, curious what this son of Nathan's would say next. Already, his first few sentences were surprisingly Nathan-like: bright, curious, and a little challenging. He'd been so passive until now that Heath had started to wonder if any of Nathan's damnable fire had passed down to him.

"I know nothing about you..." Adrien trailed off, the directness Heath had just admired disappearing behind a blush and embarrassed eyes that couldn't meet Heath's own. "I don't know anything at all."

"And yet you just experienced the most raw and vulnerable hours of your life with me," Heath offered. He reached between Adrien's legs and touched the plug there.

Adrien shuddered.

"And my cum is in your womb as we speak."

"Yes."

"And you will likely carry my child."

"All of that, yes." Adrien's throat clicked as he swallowed anxiously. "I'd feel better about all of this if I knew more about who you are. I didn't plan..." He wiped a trembling hand over his mouth and started again. "I didn't plan to auction my heat to the highest bidder. All my life I'd imagined that when the time came, I'd be in a relationship with a man who could take care of it for me, out of love and caring."

Heath said nothing. He didn't know why Adrien didn't have

a man like that if that was what he truly wanted. Alphas were eager to commit to an omega because it took the pressure off them for child care. It was in their nature, their instincts, to fall for the men who submitted to them so joyfully. It was always omegas who wanted their freedom.

His Nathan had never wanted a full commitment—he'd always loved his independence and reveled in the fact that selling his heats could fund that kind of life for him—free from responsibilities of children or running a house. It hadn't occurred to Heath that Adrien's motivations might be different.

"I didn't want to think about it…about this," Adrien went on, gesturing between them. "It was easier to put my schooling and work first and ignore that eventually I'd have to make a choice."

Heath remained silently surprised. Nathan would never have ignored an opportunity to make money, or to use his status as an omega near heat to gain entrance to society he might otherwise have been denied. Heath tried to imagine an omega with other feelings, other perspectives.

"You were afraid?" Heath asked.

Adrien nodded. "I don't know much about heat, or, well, the rest of it. My father…" He trailed off. "I never knew my omega parent."

Heath nodded. He brushed the hair back from Adrien's sweaty forehead and trailed a finger down his cheek. Adrien didn't flinch or move away from him, which softened Heath even more, and the heat crush intensified with Adrien's every unexpected word. Surprise was Heath's weakness—Nathan had always kept him guessing, shocking him at every turn. And now his son was doing the same thing—though in a completely contradictory manner.

Adrien went on, his eyes cast toward the shadows of the room as though embarrassed by his next words, "For a lot of reasons, I was never close to other omegas until I came to university, and I never thought it would be polite to ask the omega friends I've made there what to expect. It was easier to pretend it wasn't going to happen."

Heath almost laughed. Polite? What was polite about heat? Nothing. It was the exact opposite of polite, and every omega had the right to know that going in. The bruise on his heart grew, tenderness swelling in his chest for this foolish boy who'd been too afraid of being *impolite* to get the information he needed.

Adrien went on a bit tiredly, "Obviously, I should have planned better. My father always said I lived in a dream world too much. In the end, I needed the money to pay for my future." He met Heath's gaze, brows furrowed with worry. "I know the school vets you all before allowing you to participate in the auction. It's just…I want to know more than you won't kill me and you're without disease, and—" He broke off and looked around the room, confusion darkening his eyes. "—and supposedly wealthy."

Heath took a slow breath and let it out, trying to decide how much to share with Adrien given his own desire to keep a safe distance and not recklessly deepen the heat crush. "You can feel free to ask questions, but I'm also free to not answer them."

Adrien swallowed another sip of water and looked around the room. "This place is small. Given how much you paid for me, I expected something else."

"This is my heat cabin. I bring omegas here when I want to breed them."

Breeding only. Knotting and fucking during an omega's heat was another matter. Before Nathan, he'd been young and randy, and taken on omegas in heat quite regularly. Usually the omega wasn't a virgin, though, and usually he hadn't handled first heats, deeming them too expensive and troublesome. He'd only done it once before now; as a favor to his father's steward, he'd taken on his omega son's first heat. But after Nathan, Heath had been nearly abstinent, only indulging a few times but unable to tolerate the way he'd felt so close to falling for the omegas. Those interludes had taken place at one of his more remote vacation homes. This cabin was reserved for attempts at breeding. It was the place he'd been conceived, and it was the place he wanted his own child to be conceived.

"Do you do that often?" Adrien asked. "*Breed* omegas?"

"No, only twice before."

"So you have children?"

"There was a miscarriage, and the other didn't take from the start." Heath grimaced. He didn't like thinking about both failed attempts. One had been taken on with the poorest of motivations, as revenge against one of Nathan's betrayals—the bloody, awful miscarriage had seemed proper punishment for his pettiness. Luckily, the omega was still fertile and had delivered a healthy child to another alpha at his next heat. And the other breeding attempt had been instigated in his youth, a folly of infatuation with an omega he'd met just days before a heat. They'd both been lucky a child hadn't ripened.

Good God, he was a romantic fool. His life was a series of passionate mistakes. This time, for once, he'd keep his heart out of it. Transactional. He'd trade a soothing knot for the pain of growing a child and a pile of money for a piece of Nathan back in his arms.

Adrien drank more water and then whimpered, leaning back against the pillow and shuddering all over. Heath took the water glass from him and put it aside on the nightstand. It was clear Adrien had more questions, but the next heat wave was coming over him quickly.

"Don't talk now. Save it for later. Rest and get ready."

Adrien quivered and stared up at Heath with round, frightened eyes. "I don't want it. It's too much."

Heath wrapped an arm around Adrien's body, holding him in place, and then pushed down the blankets to expose his flushed body and already dripping cock. The scent of pre-cum floated up to Heath, and he licked his lips in anticipation.

"It only gets more intense from here on out," Heath whispered. "Stop resisting, little one. Give in to the ride."

Adrien cried out, his body jerking as he struggled against the rising tide of uncompromising lust. Heath kissed his throat, his cheek, his clavicles, and then sucked a nipple into his mouth.

Adrien squirmed and bucked, the understandable fear of an inexperienced omega trying to hold onto sanity during his first heat clearly gripping him. Heath rolled on top of Adrien, firmly gripping his wrists and holding them above his head.

"Give in," Heath barked. "Ride it. If you fight, it will only become monstrous."

Adrien started to sob, tears running down his face, as he tried to escape the inevitability of what was to come. "Help me," he whispered between gasping breaths. "Please. Make it stop."

"It's not going to stop," Heath said firmly, using his own hips to push Adrien's slick-wet thighs apart. "Accept it. It won't stop."

Adrien shoved and kicked, trying to get away, but Heath knew it was really the heat he fought against.

Heath released one arm, enduring pummels as he pried the plug from Adrien's ass and then positioned himself to shove inside. But before he did, he paused and said, "I'm ready to help you, little one, but you have to tell me you want my help."

"Yes, please. Help me."

"That means I fuck you. Understand? I fuck and knot you, and it helps."

"Please," Adrien begged, tears running down his face. "Just

make it stop."

"I can't." Heath tried again, finding it hard to reach the boy in his fear-soaked panic. "But I can make it better."

"Make it better. Fuck me, please."

Heath thrust inside, aiming to hit Adrien's prostate, and was gratified by the immediate orgasm that shook Adrien's body and spurted wetly between them.

"That's the only way this gets better," Heath said again, fucking into Adrien with long, hard strokes. "Submit to it. Learn to love it." He growled with pleasure and added, "You're an omega. It's your lot in life."

Adrien shuddered and came again, his eyes shining with tears and lust, the heat taking him over, body and soul.

"That's a good boy."

# Chapter Six

ADRIEN CLIMAXED FOR what felt like the hundredth time. He shook with exhaustion as the bliss of orgasm fizzled out again. He was relieved to feel Heath's knot growing inside him and relaxed as the bulbous bulge locked them together and stilled the thrusts against his prostate.

He shuddered and gulped in breaths, tears still sliding down his cheeks, as he finally calmed on Heath's knot. It was almost peaceful, save for the soft orgasms that continued to wring him out as the knot pressed relentlessly against his prostate.

Heath murmured soft words of praise and hushed him. Adrien's mind gelled slowly, coming back from the shattered space of lust and firing nerves that encompassed the rounds of heat.

Heath kissed Adrien's neck and cheek, holding him still as their bodies subsided from the relentless drive. "You're doing wonderfully," he whispered. "Has anyone ever told you how handsome you are? How delicious?"

"I've never done any of this before," Adrien reminded him, feeling pulpy, broken open, and vulnerable as all hell.

"I'm honored to be the first to see your pleasure and hold your pain." Heath sounded a little awed, and Adrien didn't know what to make of that. Moreover, he didn't understand why heats had to be like this—so much pleasure that it bled into pain, and so much pain that it turned to pleasure—but he knew that going through it with Heath wasn't as bad as he'd secretly feared. For that, he was grateful.

"You're handsome, too," Adrien admitted, softly. "Strong. Firm. Commanding." Remembering how Heath had ordered him to ride the heat, to submit, sent a shiver through him that quickly became another orgasm.

"We'll create a strong, well-made child together," Heath declared.

His weight on Adrien's was a calming balm; it locked him down in place, held him to the bed, and kept him from vanishing into the heat itself.

Heath twitched his hips, and Adrien dug his nails into Heath's shoulders, groaning as the movement shattered him again. He felt so raw, so exposed, and Heath's eyes didn't leave his face for a minute, gobbling up every expression and nuance of feeling. Adrien had never been so seen in his life.

"Your pleasure is beautiful," Heath said, and it seemed like the words almost hurt him. He rested his head on the pillow beside to Adrien, his breath puffing against Adrien's ear.

"Why did you choose me?" Adrien asked, finally, after they'd lain together for a few minutes in silent calm.

Heath hummed a non-answer.

"I'm not worth what you paid. There has to be another reason."

Heath gripped Adrien harder, thrust into him a bit more, and, once Adrien had come back down from the resulting sharp-edged orgasm, he chuckled when Adrien accused him of distraction from the question.

"Why did you choose me?" Adrien insisted, still panting and sweating from the last catapult into bliss. "Tell me. Lie if you have to, but I deserve an answer."

"Lies are a waste of everyone's time," Heath said darkly. "I chose you for personal reasons, and that's all you need to know about that."

Adrien would have liked to argue, but his skin started prickling and burning again. He went very still, fighting it.

"What did I tell you before?" Heath muttered.

"Don't fight it."

"That's right."

"But your knot's not even down yet," Adrien whined, squeezing around it in hopes that another orgasm might delay the oncoming round of heat. He shuddered and ached, but didn't get relief. "How can it be here so soon?"

Heath grunted. "You're going to have to trust me on this, but get on top so you can clench on my knot more easily."

He rolled them until Adrien was on top, straddling his thighs, his knot still holding them tied together. "Squeeze and rock," Heath said, as Adrien's chest flushed and his cheeks glowed with renewed need. "Don't fight it. Welcome it. Make it your own."

Adrien tipped his head back and groaned as he tried to do as Heath instructed. The rising heat didn't seem so demanding this time, and he hoped it would stay manageable. Otherwise, he'd be a mess, pinned on Heath's knotted cock and unable to reach satisfaction. He rocked on Heath, rotating his hips and gasping as the knot massaged his prostate.

Heath's hand wrapped around Adrien's dick, and he moaned, whimpering as Heath began to jerk him off at a steady, regular rate. The first orgasm was a kitten, purring and sharp-nailed, but the next one was a full-on tiger, and he roared when he convulsed on Heath's knot, digging his fingers into Heath's shoulders.

"That's it," Heath said with a bright avidness. "Do that again."

Adrien closed his eyes, riding Heath's knot as best as he could and shooting tiny cum loads onto Heath's belly every few minutes. The heat stayed relatively reasonable and he was able to manipulate his pleasure to keep sane. He eventually collapsed on Heath, his body worn out as the minor heat wave faded.

"That was a ripple," Heath said. "They don't happen often. Your body hasn't figured out how heats work yet. It's natural. You probably need more food." His knot was softening, and Adrien hoped it would release soon. His stomach did ache with hunger, but he was more tired than anything else.

When Heath finally pulled out, his cock left what felt like a huge vacancy behind. Adrien moaned and Heath soothed him again as he slipped the plug back in and kissed Adrien's temple. "Rest. I'll be back in a few minutes with more stew."

Adrien slipped into a dream almost immediately. He was back at school with a big belly trying to sort through a huge stack of notes he'd made on Hontu fabric dyes, but the words all seemed to be written in gibberish. He couldn't understand a word of it. Worse, the baby inside was going to come out very soon, and Lance was there asking, "How can you have him without the alpha that made him? How can you have him alone?"

"Shh, wake up." Heath's voice cut through and woke him. Adrien opened his eyes to find Heath leaning over the bed with another steaming bowl of stew. "You were having a bad dream."

Adrien rubbed at his face, his stomach growling. "How did you know?"

"You were making frightened noises." He sat down on the edge of the bed. "Sit up and eat. The next round will be here soon enough. You'll need your strength." Heath pushed the bowl into Adrien's hands.

"Do you have peanut butter?" Adrien asked, feeding himself a steaming spoonful. He wasn't so shaky this time. "And jelly? A sandwich would go great with this. Reminds me of when I was a kid and I was sick. Father always made a hearty stew and PB&J then."

Adrien spooned more of the savory warmth into his mouth, and chewed the chunks blissfully. He glanced around the room. Having grown accustomed to the dim lighting, he could now see the pictures on the walls—all woodland scenes—and a photograph on a table. He squinted toward it, trying to make it out. Two men together, but that was all he could distinguish. He ate in the quiet of the room while Heath watched without answering his questions about a sandwich.

"There," Heath said, putting the empty bowl aside on the nightstand. "We're ready for the next round. I'll make you a sandwich next time."

"Are you eating?" Adrien asked, suddenly concerned. "You need your strength, too."

Heath smiled gently. "I took a bowl while you napped. You looked too peaceful to wake at first. But then…" He shook his head. "Try to sleep some more. We don't know how long the reprieve will be for you."

Adrien tried to close his eyes, but he couldn't fall into dreams. Questions crowded his mind. So, with his eyes still shut, he asked a few. "Is this hard for you? Servicing my heat?"

Heath hesitated, and when he spoke, there was a strange timbre to his voice, something Adrien couldn't quite read, and yet he seemed to speak the truth. "The pleasure I take in you is beyond description. It's an honor to be here with you for it. Hopefully our joining will produce a child to enrich my life going onward, too."

"Honor…" Adrien hummed thoughtfully. He closed his eyes and drifted in exhausted calm, enjoying the softness of Heath's mattress. It felt much more luxurious than his hard, dorm-room pallet bed. So good on his tired back.

"Yes, an honor. And perhaps it is even a blessing to share this with you." Again with the odd tone.

Adrien opened his eyes to examine Heath. He could see him fairly clearly this close up even without his glasses. His dark beard shone glossily in the dim light, and his gray eyes were troubled. He seemed to be confused by something, but Adrien couldn't begin to guess what. His mind came back to the question of blessings, and he recalled his father calling up blessings every morning and night. Heath hadn't prayed in front of Adrien that he could recall. He asked, "Are you very religious, then?"

"Not in the least. But the word still works for nonbelievers, too. I still welcome an undeserved gift from the universe, a surprise joy to be grateful for. Gratitude isn't only for the religious among us."

"So..." Adrien cocked his head, considering. "Is every omega's heat a blessing?"

"I'd like to think so," Heath said. But the he grimaced. "Who can say? Let's leave it that I'm more grateful for this heat with you than I had anticipated."

This made no sense to Adrien. Heath had paid so much for him, more than was reasonable by any measure. What made this different for Heath? He seemed experienced; why was this heat not what he'd expected? "Because you want to breed me?"

Heath stiffened. "Because of personal reasons that I don't intend to share."

"You keep saying that. Why?" Adrien asked, raising up on his elbows, gazing steadily at Heath despite his exhaustion making that feel like a great effort.

Heath's mouth twitched, a repressed laugh. "Perhaps I like the idea of keeping some mystery."

"That's not it."

"No, it's not," Heath conceded, his voice so soft and somehow forgiving that it felt like a caress on Adrien's skin. "Now rest. No more questions, little one." He smoothed his fingers over

Adrien's forehead, and tingles broke out over Adrien's body.

Deciding to obey rather than push, Adrien drowsed, his mind supplying him with lust-soaked pseudo-dreams that kept him from falling asleep entirely. Bright memories of what he'd done with Heath kept bursting into his consciousness, along with sleepy images of things they hadn't done yet but about which Adrien had always fantasized.

Turning onto his side, the plug feeling almost natural inside of him now, he sighed heavily.

"If you can't sleep, just relax. Your body needs the rest."

Adrien opened his mouth and then closed it again.

"Yes?" Heath asked. Adrien wondered if the man would sleep at all during the heat or simply stare at him with those vigilant eyes for the whole duration.

"Will you..." Adrien blushed, not sure where the request was even coming from, only that his half-conscious mind had supplied him with the image and now he wanted to know more about it.

"Speak."

"Will you lick..." Adrien covered his face with a hand. "I can't say it."

"If you can't say it, then I can't do it," Heath said brusquely. "Rest, I said."

"Will you lick my asshole? I've never had it done, and I'd like to experience it."

Heath smiled, a white slash of teeth in his darkly stubbled face. Adrien shivered under the sharpness of it and simultaneously wanted to see it again as soon as possible. He felt praised by it. As though he'd earned a piece of Heath not usually shared.

"You want my tongue in your ass?"

Adrien squirmed, a low fire banking in his groin. His cock fattened up, and his hole squeezed around the plug. "I've never...

I've heard that it feels..." The embarrassment crept higher and higher, burning his ears and cheeks.

"Another honor," Heath declared, looming up over him.

"Should I...turn over?"

"Yes."

Adrien scrambled to get on his belly. Humiliated and excited, he buried his face in the pillow.

Heath shoved Adrien's knees apart to kneel between his thighs. Adrien groaned as Heath massaged his ass cheeks and then bent low, pressing hot, open-mouth kisses to his lower back.

As Heath spread Adrien open, he slipped out his tongue and traced it wetly down Adrien's crack. The sensation was almost ticklish, but more erotic than not, and Adrien held his breath in anticipation. As soon as Heath's tongue came to the place where the plug stoppered him, he pulled back and removed the piece.

Adrien felt the gape of his hole, and shame hit him. He didn't want to look loose and used, and he wondered if Heath would back out now.

"Beautiful," Heath growled, leaning down to tongue the rim of Adrien's gaping anus.

Adrien bucked, startled by the slick, sweet pleasure, so intense he bit down on the pillow, stifling his urge to cry out.

When Heath pressed his tongue inside, pushing against his rim and delving into his most secret place, Adrien groaned. He clung to his pillow and sobbed as Heath took the time to tongue-fuck him, slowly and with a firm deliberateness that could not be denied.

Adrien felt the next round of heat rising up in him. He lifted his head enough to grunt, "Here it comes, sir." The honorific gliding from his lips unbidden.

And then it was on him.

The world dissolved into a golden-hued need to get fucked

and come.

He must have begged, because when Heath shoved into him, he leaned low over Adrien's back and whispered, "Don't beg, little one. I'm here."

And was he ever.

Adrien felt full to the brim, but he needed to be so much fuller. Only Heath's knot would do. He arched frantically into the fuck, reaching behind to claw at Heath's shoulders, whining high in his throat.

"Calm down," Heath ordered. "Let me take care of you."

Adrien moaned, his body surrendering to the violence of Heath's thrusts. He quaked through orgasms, shouted his pleasure and fear, and let himself go deep into heat-thrall. Awash in lust and need, riding Heath's plunging cock and cresting into ecstasy, Adrien only calmed again when Heath bellowed his own climax and his knot began to swell.

As Heath crooned softly to him, Adrien rocked himself to sleep against the massive pressure in his ass.

HEATH HELD ADRIEN as he slept, his knot tying them together. He closed his eyes and tried to sleep, too, but the damn heat crush tore at his peacefulness. He mentally reviewed all the heats he'd ever handled in his life, purposely skipping over the memories of Nathan's because they'd always been fraught. Yes, with every heat his heart softened toward the omega, sometimes uncomfortably so, and after Nathan's death that terrible tendency had led to him walking away from taking on omega's heats. But never had his heart felt quite like this.

He wasn't sure what to make of it. He felt affectionate, yes, and what alpha wouldn't when Adrien had submitted so beautifully, and, after a fearful start, given in to his body's needs so enthusiastically? He could place the blame for the additional draw he felt toward Adrien at the feet of his resemblance to Nathan, but that didn't fully encompass it either.

Each moment with Adrien felt entirely different from the heats he'd handled with Nathan. Those had always been infused with a terror and hurt, a submission to Nathan's whims and needs that Heath had hardly understood. Ostensibly, he'd always been the alpha—the one to care for, nurture, and knot Nathan—but he'd never *felt* like the alpha. He'd felt like a supplicant, begging for Nathan's approval, for his affection, for his love.

With Adrien, despite his superficial likeness to Nathan, the experience was entirely different. He was the alpha and felt it in his bones: dominant, commanding, and in control. He felt strong, passionate, and protective. He felt all the things he'd always wanted to be for Nathan, but had never been allowed to display. Even with the other omegas he'd handled, including the two he'd bred, he'd always been at their mercy, determined to protect their interests. His omega parent had been a fierce proponent of omega rights, and Heath had internalized those messages: allow omegas to set the standards for the heat, follow their guidelines and let them take the lead.

There hadn't been any such discussion beforehand with Adrien, what with Heath having been determined to keep the relationship transactional and Adrien being too innocent to know that he should, or even could, draw lines and boundaries, make demands of what the alpha could and couldn't do, to the extent of making Heath gain consent before every position change.

No, Adrien had come to the heat cabin blindly, and Heath had allowed him to do that because he hadn't wanted to cede control this time. He'd ignorantly thought that by taking command he could control his heart, and thus had been shocked by the heat crush when it began, and was swamped by it now that the heat was in full swing.

Adrien's surrender was so complete that Heath couldn't help but fall in love with it, even if his feelings for the boy—no, the man—himself were unexplored and untested, unknowable while they churned and fucked in the throes of heat. But that surrender? That was something he could fall for, and he had. Oh, how he had fallen for it.

If this were Nathan he was fucking, he'd think it was a trick. But Adrien was guileless and didn't seem to understand the way an alpha responded to a beautiful omega in full submission, the way it made them want to beat their chest and roar, or claim the flesh displayed with abandon as their own, or fuck it full of babies to raise together in a safe, private home, far away from the meddling world.

His head rushed, blue and black dots flickered before his eyes, and he realized he'd been holding his breath. He let it out slowly, held tighter to Adrien, and tried to calm the traitorous beat of his soft, open heart. He wanted to close it off again, to protect himself from the potential pain of loving…but he couldn't just yet. Once the heat crush was over, he could harden himself again.

And if there ended up being a pregnancy to get through together then he'd have to find another way to keep his distance and his heart intact. If there was one thing Nathan had taught him, it was that loving was never safe.

# Chapter Seven

THE DAYS PASSED by in the tight-handed grip of pleasure, punctuated by a few hours of sleep and Heath supplying water and stew. Adrien felt lost to the heaving cycles of heat, thinking of nothing else, his mind a canvas painted over in the colors of erotic sensation only.

Eventually, the lulls between the cycles grew longer again, the hours of sleep deeper, and finally his appetite returned full force. Waking to a dim room, and with no sense of what time or day it was, Adrien sat up straight in bed and proclaimed, "I'm hungry."

Heath stretched and sat up beside him. "You must be ravenous. You were so demanding in your needs that it became hard to keep you nourished."

Adrien's embarrassment forced him to look away, though he was secretly incredibly impressed by Heath's darkly furred chest.

"Never be ashamed of your natural inclinations." Heath gripped Adrien's chin, gazing down into his eyes. "You were a perfect omega, and your surrender was beautiful to witness." He kissed Adrien's mouth softly and then pulled back as though he'd surprised himself. "Wait here. I'll be right back with something to eat, and then we'll see if you're steady enough to make it to the shower."

Adrien watched as Heath climbed out of bed, naked skin on display as it had been for the last several days, and he shivered as he took in for the first time how thickly muscled Heath's thighs and arms were, and his chest and shoulders, too. How had he missed that while being fucked by the man? Heat was a mesmerizing thing.

"Here," Heath said, striding back in the room.

"No more stew," Adrien murmured, rubbing at his eyes in order to avoid being confronted with Heath's full-frontal nudity and his swinging dick. It was ridiculous to be so reticent now. He'd had the man inside of him, begged for his knot, and was currently plugged up with the semen from their last bout. And yet...

Heath climbed into the bed beside him. "Fruit. Fresh strawberries. Melon. Orange slices."

Adrien's mouth watered, and he scooted close, taking the proffered bowl from Heath's hands. The sweet and tart flavors spangled over his tongue as he scarfed down the contents of the bowl. "Thank you. This is so good."

"Do you need more?"

Nodding, Adrien waited as Heath took off back to the kitchen and returned with another bowl of fruit. After eating that second helping just as quickly, he was finally satisfied. He smiled up at Heath hopefully. "Now what?"

"Let's shower," Heath said, taking the empty bowl from him. "Then you'll want to see daylight. It's been almost a week."

Adrien nodded, letting Heath lead him to the bathroom by the hand. A brief flash of modesty struck him, a memory of his father telling him to always cover up, but he ignored it. There was a shimmering, shy sense of rightness in being naked for Heath now. Especially when Heath turned to smile at him as he cranked on the water in the plain, white-tiled room. "You're steady?"

"Yes." Adrien's stomach fluttered, a flock of butterflies rising in response to the brightness of Heath's teeth in his dark beard.

"You did wonderfully," Heath said, sitting on the edge of the tub, tenderness in his tone that tugged at Adrien's spent balls. If he could get hard again after the days of constant sexual activity, that quality in Heath's voice would do it for him. Heath tested the water with one hand before shaking the excess from his fingers and reaching toward Adrien. "I'm proud of you. Such a strong, beautiful, sexy man."

Adrien swallowed hard, his cock thickening almost painfully. Heath's smile broadened, and he took Adrien's hardness in hand, then bent to kiss the tip gently. "You are deliciously responsive." He looked up at Adrien then, as though assessing something important. "You do everything I ask of you and more."

"It felt right to please you. It still does."

Heath's jaw worked a moment and then he replied huskily, "You deserve a final reward."

Adrien was about to ask about the word 'final' when Heath opened up and sucked him in deep. He moaned. His flesh was sensitive all over, a nervous, exhausted feeling, but his cock in Heath's mouth felt wonderful. Bathed by Heath's tongue and stoked by the soft inside of his cheeks as he sucked, Adrien gave in to the surprising pleasure.

He closed his eyes, gripped Heath's hair, and then sobbed as an orgasm fluttered through him, like a shadow of the intense orgasms of heat. He whimpered and gazed in glassy-eyed wonder as Heath swallowed the small load he'd produced and kissed the head of his dick again.

"Sweet," Heath said softly. "Like the rest of you."

The water was warm and steaming up the room. Heath guided Adrien beneath the stream before following him into the shower. "You're wobbly after everything," Heath murmured softly. "It's my job to keep you safe."

Adrien surrendered to Heath's touch, letting him wash him with a cloth and soap, and then suds up his hair, too. The plug stayed tight inside, improving the chance of conception, and Heath washed around it, too. By the time the shower was over, Adrien was both rejuvenated and drained, and all he wanted to do was find a quiet place to sit where he could see the sky and breathe. Maybe eat again, too. Something heartier than fruit this time.

His stomach growled in agreement.

HEATH WAS LOATHE to admit it even to himself, but he couldn't deny he was sorry Adrien's heat had come to an end. And not just because he wasn't sure if he would ever again have the privilege to witness the beguiling way Adrien's throat arched when he cried out with pleasure, or the fragile vulnerability of his innocence, or the wide-eyed faith he demonstrated as he clung to Heath while they rode the heat cycles together. It was because when Heath was in Adrien's presence he felt himself complete: an alpha, a man, a lover. He thrived on what Adrien gave him effortlessly, a priceless thing that he handed over like it was as simple as breathing. A gift Nathan had never expressed: trust. Complete and utter, boundless, unrestrained, and unreasonable trust.

With every moment, Adrien's resemblance to Nathan faded away, replaced by the stunning transparency of his soul, the complete lack of machinations, and the sense that his future was still so unwritten, so blank and open. So potentially Heath's.

Alone in the bathroom, Heath took his time dressing and considered what he was going to do now. The heat had passed, but his crush remained. The desire to protect and pleasure, to discover more about the sweet puzzle of a man he'd only started to know clawed at his insides like a predator. There was nothing innocent about the feeling.

Zipping his jeans, he turned to the mirror and combed his dark hair as he tried to think his way out of what he knew he needed to do. He didn't want to say goodbye today. He hated the thought of giving Adrien up now that he'd had him. Not even for a few weeks while they waited to see if the breeding took.

But that was the agreement, and it was written into the contract per Heath's original wishes to keep it all transactional, to keep his distance and preserve his heart. Damn, but his heart was definitely in danger. There was no doubt about that. Heath's hand shook as he continued to brush his hair. Adrien wasn't Nathan, he reminded himself. Nathan was a different kind of omega entirely.

But he'd originally insisted on the more liberal contract that allowed a bred omega to return to their life as they awaited signs of pregnancy. The idea being that until a pregnancy was confirmed, it benefited the omega to get back to their work, school, or whatever else. Traditionally, omegas stayed with alphas until pregnancy was confirmed or denied, but omega rights had changed all that. Therefore, Heath and Adrien's contract made it clear: unless Adrien was carrying Heath's child, his progeny, he would never have any rights over Adrien again.

Heath dropped the comb to the bathroom sink and stared at himself in the mirror. What a fool he'd been. He smiled grimly, not sure what he'd been more foolish about: believing he could keep affection for Adrien out of his heart or failing entirely to do so.

It had been less than twenty-four hours since the last cycle had hit, but Heath was contractually obligated to accept that it was time for Adrien to go.

The knock on the bathroom door brought him out of his reverie.

"Can I get dressed now?" Adrien called through the wood.

"It's almost time for me to go."

Heath jerked the door open and took one last look at Adrien's lean body, and he still ached to fatten him up. "Yes," he said, gruff and irritable that he had no choice but to agree. "And hurry."

Watching Adrien put clothes on again for the first time since he'd taken them off in front of the cabin was like having a tooth drilled without Novocain. It took all of his willpower not to reach out to Adrien and demand that he stay, order him to get those awful clothes off his body and climb back in bed where he belonged.

But he restrained himself, forcing a close-lipped smile, before saying, "Drive carefully. You might be carrying my child."

Adrien swallowed hard, pushing up the glasses Heath had let him don again after the rage of the heat was over. "I will."

They left the cabin and stepped out into the bright light of day.

They stared at each other as the birds cawed and swooped overhead. The trees rustled and swayed in the forest around them, and the house stood behind him like an empty, cavernous maw, devoid of anything but echoes of recent joy.

"Um, so, thanks," Adrien said quietly. He licked his lips and looked down at the ground and then up at Heath again. "For, you know…"

"Buying your heat?"

"Yeah, and for being so nice."

"Was I nice?" Heath asked. He remembered ordering Adrien to the ground outside and then rough-fucking him in the entryway. He regretted that treatment now.

"You were…" Adrien glanced away and then seemed to force himself to meet Heath's eyes again. "You were what I needed. Thank you for taking charge."

"Anytime." He meant it, too. He'd take charge again right now if he thought Adrien truly wanted him to. There was a glimmer in the boy's eye that made him wonder…but, no, he'd follow the contracts to the letter. There was every reason to hope the breeding would take, and then he'd have over a year of Adrien at his side. He could get to know every inch of Adrien inside and out, find out what made him tick, discover what motivated a young man like him. Learn the scent and look of him in every season. There was no reason to push it now.

Well, aside from the growing sense of despair at the thought of Adrien getting into his car and driving away. The impending loss reminded him of how he'd felt after Nathan died. Not so soul-wrenching, but a similar imprint of pain, just enough that it was horribly familiar.

"I guess I should go," Adrien said, scuffing his tennis shoes on the ground.

*You don't have to*, Heath almost said, but he kept his mouth tightly closed on the words.

"I'll, uh, I guess I'll be in touch. About how it goes. If the breeding took or not. I should know in a week or so."

Heath nodded.

Adrien chewed on his bottom lip. "Before I leave, though, I wanted to ask one more thing."

"What's that?"

"Would you kiss me?"

Heath grunted and took two long strides forward, grabbed Adrien by the waist, and kissed him hard and possessively. He tasted the boy's tongue and plunged deeper, taking ownership of his mouth. Then he released him, his heart pounding and his throat working to keep from demanding that Adrien stay.

"Thank you," Adrien whispered, his lips red from their kiss. "I'm glad it was you."

He broke out of Heath's arms like he was in some kind of rush, jumped into his car, and started it. He pulled away down the drive, kicking up dust and leaves behind him.

Heath stared after him, stood his ground and let the surrounding forest soothe his sense of loss.

# PART TWO

## Pregnancy

# Chapter Eight

THE DAYS FOLLOWING Adrien's first heat were covered in a strange sense of unreality. He walked through the world as though barely tethered to it. Some vital part of himself remained behind in Heath's heat cabin, and only his shell went about his day-to-day life.

For the third day in a row, he sat at his desk in the campus's old art building staring at the latest swatches of the Hontu fabric he was studying. The patterns were as bright as ever, the design as flawless, and the mystery of meaning just as deeply hidden within the heart of the fabric itself, but he couldn't seem to summon a passion for it. Today, he held an orange and blue swath, noting that it demonstrated a more evenly battened weft than any he'd previously studied, but he couldn't focus his mind long enough to start a list of investigative questions. Even wondering "why this change?" and "how this change?" didn't come to him.

He rested his chin in his hand and growled at his own lack of focus. After a few more minutes of staring at the new fabric, he put it aside, and spoke sternly to himself. "What's wrong with you? You did this so you could stay in school and continue on to become a professor. You're ambitious and intelligent, remember? Get it together."

But no matter how he argued with himself, his mind wandered until he finally abandoned his desk and left his work behind in order to return to the comparative nest of his room.

"How's it going?" Lance asked, falling into stride beside him on the sidewalk outside the art building.

"All right," Adrien muttered. He wanted to get back to his room and curl up in his bed. He missed the stew Heath had fed him, though he couldn't say why. When he'd first finished the heat, he'd thought he'd never want to taste it again. Now it seemed like the only thing that would satisfy him.

Lance clucked his tongue. "I don't buy that, friend. In fact, I'd say you've seemed sort of down since you got back."

"Is that unusual?" Adrien asked, stopping in his tracks. He didn't know how he was supposed to feel or behave after having turned himself over to someone like Heath, but he felt disoriented and lost. And a little ashamed. Not of what he'd done, or what they'd shared, but that he couldn't seem to get his act together now that he was back at school. Heath had bid on him because he was ambitious. Where was his ambition now? Fucked away in a week?

He took hold of Lance's arm and said, "Is there something wrong with me?"

"I don't know. Maybe." He grinned. "But for someone who earned a ton of money for his first heat, I'd have expected you'd have a bit more spring in your step. Think of all you can do with your life now. All the places you could travel! The things you could see!"

"Hmm." Adrien released Lance's arm, pushed his glasses up his nose, and shrugged. "I guess."

Lance's eyebrows nearly hit his hairline, but all he said was, "Want to talk about it?"

"I don't know how," Adrien said. "It was the most important thing that ever happened to me, and I shared it with a guy I barely know. It feels like it was all a dream."

But that wasn't accurate at all. It felt like his *life* now was the dream. The heat cabin and all the scents, sensations, and pleasures of it seemed the only real thing in the world. Lance even struck him as strangely false. All he really wanted to think about now was Heath. Where was he? What was he doing and who was he with? Did Heath think of him at all? Did he miss him? Or had Heath simply moved on with his life as though the heat cabin had never happened, only caring whether the breeding had taken?

They started walking again toward the dorm, and Adrien was glad to be moving. It helped him focus to know that he would be back in his bed soon, where he could sleep and dream of the heat cabin.

"Have you talked to the guy who won your heat? You know, since you got back?" Lance asked. "Sometimes that helps, you know. With the post-heat separation, that is."

"Post-heat separation?"

"You went through an intense bonding experience. Literally, if you're pregnant. Like, the two of you are bonded together into another life. In fact, I'd say your state of mind right now leads me to think you *are* pregnant, and that it did take."

Adrien palmed his flat stomach. He didn't feel any different, aside from this morose disinterest in his former life and a deep yearning for Heath. "It's too soon to know."

"Maybe, but I've seen it before. I'm the oldest of six, remember? I've seen how both my step-omegas acted after they got knocked up during heats. If it didn't take, they shook off the post-heat melancholy easily. If they were growing a new life inside, they turned inward and got really dependent on my father. The worst was the time they were both pregnant simultaneously. I thought my father would lose his mind. But that's another story."

Adrien didn't want to be dependent on anyone. And yet he couldn't help but recall how nice it had felt to be hand-fed by

Heath, cared for, and bathed. He could put up with some more of that quite happily.

Lance grinned. "I guess we'll know by the end of the week, huh?"

"I suppose we will."

"And what happens if you *are* pregnant?" Lance asked as they approached the dormitory. "What did you agree on?"

"I go to live with him until the baby is born and then, assuming I'm happy there, I'm to remain for one year of chestfeeding."

Lance nodded. "I'm gonna miss you around here."

Adrien touched his stomach again. "You're that certain, huh?"

"I'm pretty damn sure. You've got the 'growing baby' blues." He took Adrien's arm and led him toward the elevators in the lobby. As they rode up to Lance's floor, he said, "Don't worry. It passes into 'hormonally hellish' horniness before too long."

"What's that supposed to mean?"

"Oh, give it a few weeks. You'll see. And then you'll understand why my dad nearly died when dealing with two at the same time." Lance waggled his eyebrows and broke away as the elevator dinged. "See you later, Mr. Preggo."

Adrien flipped him the bird.

# Chapter Nine

A WEEK LATER, Adrien was packing his bags, jittery with anticipation and worry. Ron Finch and two other employees from the university matcher service were in his dorm room helping him box up his things, explaining what to expect, and what the university promised him in terms of his future return to the school after the baby was born and the chestfeeding completed.

"Your position here is guaranteed. That's part of the charm of using the university matcher service. So, once the baby is weaned from chestfeeding, you can return to school and pick up right where you left off!"

Adrien didn't bother to point out the inaccuracy of that. Some of his work was time sensitive and would be passed on to others to finish. But he'd known that when he'd agreed to do the auction and offered up the breeding as an extra. He'd have to find a new topic of research when he came back. A prick of disappointment momentarily soured his relief that he'd see Heath again soon, but that was soon washed away in a flood of wild anticipation.

A dark-haired older man whose name Adrien didn't recall motioned toward the last box and said, "These will be delivered to your alpha's address within the next forty-eight hours. So be sure to pack anything you definitely need in the meantime in your suitcase."

Adrien nodded. He wasn't an idiot. He'd already thought of that. Besides, he just wanted to get on the road. The anticipation and apprehension was overwhelming. He knew the drive was about four hours, and he was already aching from head-to-toe to see Heath again. But what about Heath? Would he be happy to see Adrien, too? What would it be like between them without the heat drawing them together? What would a year in a stranger's house really mean? There were too many questions he didn't know the answer to. The whole world felt like it was on the verge of being reborn, and he didn't have any idea what form it would take.

Besides, he wanted to see Heath's face, to judge his reaction to the news of a baby for himself.

Adrien hadn't been the one to inform Heath of the pregnancy, unfortunately. Ron Finch had taken that job as his own, claiming it was the way it was always done. He said it marked the official conclusion of the auction since at that time he'd taken the payment in full on Adrien's behalf—including the pregnancy bonus. Adrien had to take Ron's word when he said that Heath was pleased.

But Adrien told himself Heath *must* be happy about the baby. After all, Heath had paid a great deal of money for the option of breeding him, and he'd seemed determined to ensure he would get pregnant by keeping him plugged for the duration of the heat. Still, there was something inside him insisting that he *had* to see Heath's face and hear him say he was happy for himself. And the sooner the better.

He only had to stop twice to vomit during the drive, and he supposed that was a success given that he'd been puking a lot more often than he'd like over the last few days. He hoped this stage would pass quickly, because he was pretty sure that Heath wouldn't find vomit very appealing in an omega.

As he came over the mountain ridge on the main road, he saw the glitter of the city spreading out before him. Wellport, resting by the sea and serving as the seat of government for the nation, fairly screamed wealth. High-rises reached for the sky, as their residents reached for the upper echelons of power. The best neighborhoods in the city were old money, and some of the finest homes were built alongside the large parks intended for the enjoyment of the original founding families back in the 'days of yore.' And a few of the nicest homes were built within the parks themselves.

That's where Heath's home resided, inside one such park, called Clearwood. And, according to the directions provided by the university, the house was referred to as Clearwood Castle. Adrien wasn't certain what to make of that. The Heath he'd been impregnated by had seemed content in a tiny cabin in the woods. This Heath of Wellport and Clearwood Castle seemed like a dark mystery.

Dear God, did he even know the man's last name? He didn't think he did. He'd never asked.

Locating Clearwood Park was easy enough. The winding, meandering roads through the grounds showed off flowering greenways, spacious lawns, and lushly wooded parkland. As he drove through, Adrien's anxiety began to ease. Yes, this seemed to be the kind of place that the Heath he'd met, the man he'd gone through his heat with, would choose to live. Close to nature, away from the chaos of the big city, but somehow close enough that he could still get to work—whatever that might entail, Adrien was still unsure—in under an hour.

The gate marking the driveway from the park was thick and made of iron. As Adrien pulled up in front of it, peering into the wooded distance, he could just make out the top of what looked like a rather astonishingly large stone house. He was just wondering how he was going to get inside when the gate swung slowly open on its own. He shoved away the resurgence of nerves as he drove slowly through.

When the house came into view, Adrien gulped down the shock of saliva in his mouth, and stared, gobsmacked, at the castle-like structure looming in front of him. The front of the building showed off turrets and rooflines that took his breath away, and the stone itself was laid in a pattern that left Adrien feeling as though he'd walked into a fairytale book. Or driven, rather. Since he still hadn't left his car.

The massive wooden front doors, shaped like those on a medieval castle, opened, and Adrien's breath stuttered as Heath stepped outside. He was smoothly shaved, wore a dark suit and sleek tie, polished black shoes, and a serious expression that turned Adrien's guts inside out and his heart upside down. He tried to breathe but found he couldn't grab a full breath as he worked to unbuckle his seat belt.

Where was the gruff man from the woods? Where were his beard and his soft T-shirt and blue jeans? Who was this man? Adrien's fingers froze on the door handle, and he had to talk himself into getting out. This was what he'd agreed to, what he'd wanted up until this very moment. He took a deep breath and let it out. As he climbed from the car, two servants darted forward from the shadows of the house and began to collect his things. Adrien blinked at them, resettled his glasses, and stared up at the house again.

He was supposed to live here? Until the baby came?

All around them the woods sang with birdsong. It was hard to imagine that the sparkling city, with all its people and cars, all its stores and shows, was just a short drive away. Clearwood Castle felt completely isolated. And that, at least, was familiar to Adrien. That felt right. It was the imposing nature of the place, the darkness of the stone, and the smooth presentation of its master that had him undone and unsure.

He wiped his hands against his jeans and wished he'd worn something other than a rock 'n' roll T-shirt he'd purchased at a very loud stadium concert last autumn.

Once the servants were back inside, taking all of Adrien's luggage with them, Heath stepped forward. The intent expression in his gray eyes was so like the one he'd worn when Adrien had arrived at the heat cabin that Adrien's hands went to the button on his jeans, anticipating that Heat would command him to bend over and show his hole again.

"It's intimidating, I know," Heath said finally. The rasp of his voice shivered up and down Adrien's spine, and he felt his nipples harden in response. Was he trained to react to this man now? Or was it what Lance had said? Pregnancy hormones making him horny?

Adrien tried to concentrate. "This is your home?"

"Ancestral, yes," Heath said. "My great-great-great-grandfather Clearwood built it when Wellport was simply 'the port' and barely a skyscraper blemished the sky."

Adrien's hand still lingered on his jeans button. Heath's gaze strayed down to it, and his mouth, no longer hidden behind a beard, smirked slightly.

"Come inside," he said, turning on his heel without touching Adrien at all—no welcoming hug or handshake. No kiss. A stab of disappointment pierced him. What had he expected though? Just like at the heat cabin, he was out of his depth. "I've prepared an area for your stay. It's roomy but cozy at the same time. You'll be safe there."

Adrien followed Heath up the great stone stairs and into a massive, shadowy hall adorned with marble statues, oil paintings, and a large, ornate, and somehow terrifying clock made from giant slabs of carved wood and sharp metal pieces. The hands showed it to be midafternoon. He'd spent more time puking on the side of the road than he'd thought.

"This way," Heath said, his shoulders stiff and his gait rapid. Adrien had to hurry to keep up.

His glasses slipped again and again as anxious perspiration slid down the side of his face. They rushed through wide hallways, bypassing open doors that led to rooms that seemed to serve various functions for the household. Then, suddenly, they passed through a door that partitioned the front of the house off from the back, and immediately all was different. They'd entered into a concrete tunnel, and yet somehow it felt lighter and airy, with wide windows on the upper half and skylights that channeled sunlight in from every angle.

Adrien looked around in wonder and risked reaching out to touch the concrete, finding it cool to the touch.

"In the winter, the walls are warm," Heath said without turning, as though he'd somehow sensed Adrien's curiosity. "There is an oven for this part of the house, and the heat from it follows paths through the concrete, warming them from the inside out."

"They're cold now."

"In the summer, the same paths are connected to a chilly underground stream. It keeps the rooms cool."

"Impressive."

"Thank you."

Then nothing more was said as Heath led them deeper. Eventually, Heath stopped in front of a door and gestured down the tunnel. "That leads to the common rooms and the garden." He opened the door and motioned for Adrien to step inside. "This will be your bedroom, and you can leave your things here."

The bedroom was made entirely of glass walls. The brown and green of the woods from the park seemed to encroach, and yet the skylights brought sunlight in from above. It felt like being outside and inside all at once. Adrien stared around in amazement.

"I hope you like it," Heath said quietly, his voice still doing something to Adrien's insides that he didn't understand. "Make yourself comfortable."

Just outside one of the massive glass walls was a bubbling brook, and next to the brook were swaying trees and a view that funneled deep into the forest of the park.

"This is..."

"Private," Heath said. "There is a kitchen and living room down the hall. You'll see one servant and me. Otherwise, you'll be safe and alone here to grow the baby."

"Alone?" Adrien frowned. "I'm a prisoner?"

Heath tilted his head, concern flashing over his face. "Even after you were confirmed pregnant, did no one explain to you how it will be, Adrien? How *you* will be?"

"I..." Adrien trailed off.

"You felt it would be impolite to ask?" Heath's voice held a note of teasing, but exasperation too.

"No. Yes. I...don't know a lot about pregnancy. The conservative religious school my father sent me to when he was still alive preached that heat and pregnancy was for the alpha to understand and the omega to experience. I never rectified that gap when I was in university for reasons I already explained to you."

Heath snorted softly.

"I'm sorry. I didn't know there were things I should know." Adrien closed his eyes. He sounded like an idiot. How could he have just assumed that once he was with Heath everything would make sense again? He must seem so foolish.

"No one told you anything at all? Not the university matcher?"

"He probably assumed I already knew. My friend Lance said that I would be..." He cleared his throat. "Horny."

Heath's smirk returned. "It's not like heat. But you'll desperately want me to take you."

Adrien's cock twitched and his asshole spasmed. Truth be told, he wanted Heath to take him now. Take him and make him forget everything about the pregnancy, about this 'castle,' and every single question and fear that now grew steadily inside him.

"You're close to begging already," Heath said, nodding. "I sense how you want me."

Adrien raised his gaze to Heath's face. "No one told me how it would be," he confessed. "But I trust you to do what's best for me." He didn't know why, couldn't explain it, but the words tumbled out of him honest and strange.

Heath went very still, and Adrien almost thought he'd said something wrong. Then he ordered, "Then take off your clothes. You'll be naked for the rest of your stay."

Adrien blinked. "But—"

"Do as I say." Heath's eyes shone with authority. "Now."

"My glasses, too?"

"You can keep the glasses on while you're here. Or leave them off. Whatever makes you most comfortable."

Adrien's hands shook, but he didn't know if it was with fear or lust. He tugged off his T-shirt and unbuttoned his jeans, toed off his tennis shoes and socks, and got naked quickly. He hesitated, considering his glasses. Without them he wouldn't see as clearly, but he set them aside for now anyway. When he straightened, his cock bobbed up against his stomach.

An urge to cover his abdomen with his hands, to protect the baby inside, passed over him, but he didn't. Instead, he stood with shaking limbs as Heath gazed at him and then motioned for him to turn around. "Slowly," Heath said. "Let me see you."

Adrien spun, taking in the blurry bed with white sheets, the entertainment unit with a TV, laptop, and what looked like gaming consoles, and the shelves and shelves of books against the wall. There was another smaller door that seemed to lead to a bathroom. His heart was pounding when he faced Heath again.

"Have you been eating? You look thinner."

"I've been sick, sir. Vomiting. Because of the baby."

Heath's hard expression softened, and he stepped closer. The rustle of his suit, and the stark contrast between Adrien's nakedness and Heath's layers of clothing, appealed in a sensual way, and he wanted more than anything for Heath to take him into his arms, so he could rub his body all over his alpha's expensive suit.

"You'll feel better now that you're with me," Heath said firmly.

Adrien didn't know if that was a fact, something to do with alpha pheromones and their effect on omegas, or simply an unreasonable alpha command from Heath, so he only nodded. Adrien's hips arched forward as Heath drew near enough to smell—vetiver and whiskey—so warm, earthy, and right. His cock flexed hard and dribbled pre-cum onto the hardwood floor between them. Heath gazed at where it puddled on the ground.

"Get on your knees," Heath said, his voice gravelly and rough.

Adrien didn't need to be told twice. His mouth was already watering with the desire to pleasure Heath, to taste his cock and swallow his cum. He shivered as Heath ran his fingers into Adrien's hair and gazed down at him. The hardwood floor dug into Adrien's knees, but he didn't care. His cock didn't care either, tensing again, and leaving more goo on the floor.

He felt his asshole leak slick. Not gush, like when he was in heat, but a dribble that left no room for pretending he didn't want Heath to slide his fat, wide alpha cock up there and make him come on his dick.

"You're beautiful," Heath said calmly. "So trusting. So delicious. And mine."

"Yours," Adrien repeated, and then his hand did come to his stomach, touching where he knew the baby was growing every day. "We're yours."

Heath growled and wrenched open his pants. The evidence of his arousal pleased Adrien in a soul-deep way, and he opened his mouth greedily, leaning forward to suck the crown of Heath's cock, swallowing the slippery tang of his pre-cum.

"Yes," Heath whispered. "Suck it."

Adrien closed his eyes. He sucked and bobbed, he tongued and worked, wrapping his hand around the base of Heath's dick and jerking him until he got a nice squirt of pre-cum in his mouth. Then he moaned, pulled off, and rolled the flavor around greedily.

"Oh, sweet one," Heath grunted. "You love it."

Adrien nodded. He did; he loved the taste of Heath. It satisfied him like no food had since he'd left Heath's heat cabin. He opened his mouth for more, sucking Heath down hungrily, opening his throat and gagging on his wide, hard cock.

"Get ready," Heath moaned, thrusting into Adrien's throat, slapping his balls against Adrien's chin. "Swallow it. Every drop."

Adrien grunted and nodded, hanging onto Heath's hips. Adrien's senses were filled with the musky aroma of his skin and arousal. Heath plunged deep, gripping Adrien's hair and choking him with his cock. Adrien gagged and struggled, but when the first burst of semen shot into his gullet, he relaxed and gave in, trying to swallow it down, wanting every single bit of Heath's pleasure deep in his stomach.

As the shouting ended and Heath ripped his cock out of Adrien's throat, he gasped for air, sucking in oxygen madly. He groaned as Heath very gently wiped the saliva from his chin.

"That was good," Heath said calmly. "That will settle your stomach, too."

Adrien blinked up at him, dazed and harder than he could remember being since the heat. He wanted to jerk off, but something about Heath's gaze on him kept him still for the time being.

"You're not a prisoner," Heath said steadily, holding Adrien's chin and staring into his eyes. His cock was still hard, and it bobbed, wet and slick, in front of Adrien's face. He reached out his tongue and licked the head of it. Heath hissed and released Adrien's chin to put his cock away and fasten his suit pants again. When he looked impeccable once more, he turned his gaze back to Adrien at his feet. He stroked Adrien's cheek and said, again, "You're not a prisoner. But there's a reason you don't see pregnant omegas on the street."

Adrien blinked up at him. It was true. He'd never seen a pregnant omega in his life outside of the few educational films and pictures in books that had been part of his meager omega sex ed class. How strange that had never struck him before now.

"You'll be growing quickly. Clothing will be uncomfortable. Your body will be preparing for birth. You'll drip slick and you'll lactate—make milk—even before the baby comes. And you'll be like this"—Heath gestured at Adrien's hard cock—"anytime I'm near you. Which is why there will be times when I give you a break and let a servant care for your non-sexual needs, like bringing your meals and cleaning up your space. That's for your welfare and the health of the baby—so you can concentrate enough to eat something aside from me."

Adrien licked his lips, his eyes going back to Heath's crotch, wishing for another few spurts of his semen. Nothing had ever tasted so good. He desperately wanted more.

Heath smiled down at him. "You are still such a filthy, cock-hungry slut for me. Worth every cent for your mouth alone."

Adrien blinked up at him, dazed and still achingly hard. He smiled. "Thank you."

"Now take hold of yourself, and stare into my eyes. I want to watch your face when you come."

Adrien wanted to beg Heath to touch him, to finger his ass-hole and then fuck him mercilessly, but he couldn't look away from Heath's commanding gaze, so he did as he was told. He took his hard prick in hand and worked it quickly, staring at Heath's gray eyes as he did. He watched the shade change, growing darker with renewed lust, and when he felt the charge in his balls, the oncoming rapture of orgasm, he struggled to keep his eyes open and fixed to Heath's, but he managed.

"Please!" Adrien cried as the cum surged up his shaft. "Fuck me, sir! Please!"

"I'll fuck you, Adrien," Heath said, his voice dark with promise. "Tonight. You'll be so full of me, I'll take you so deep that you'll taste me in your mouth."

Adrien cried out, his cum striping over Heath's shiny shoes, white and slick and copious. His back arched and his hips pumped forward, as shot after shot of come flew from his swollen cockhead. He felt his womb clench inside, balling up hard in response to his orgasm, and the tension of that and the teeth-rattling pleasure left him spent and exhausted at Heath's feet.

One of Heath's hands threaded into his hair, and the other gently trailed over Adrien's ear, touching the shell and then the lobe before releasing him. "That was beautiful," Heath said. "Normally, I'd have you lick the cum from my shoes, but I don't want to risk your health with germs or bacteria." He smiled softly. "You have my child in your body. We have to be careful with him."

Adrien nodded, eyes bleary. He panted and ached, suddenly horribly tired.

"Crawl into bed," Heath said, as though reading his mind. He guided Adrien into the soft, fluffy whiteness. "Get comfortable. Rest."

Adrien's eyes drooped, but he kept them open, marking the contrast between the rough nature outside the window and the sleek suit on Heath.

"I'll send Simon to make dinner after you've had time to nap." He ran fingers through Adrien's hair, making him sleepier. He spoke like he was telling a bedtime story, soothing and calm. "Then, tonight, after my meeting in the city, I'll come here and pleasure you until you pass out."

Adrien shivered with anticipation, his cock twitching with interest despite the intense orgasm he'd just had. It wasn't heat; it wasn't compulsory, but it was a lush, heady need all the same.

Heath went on, "This will be your life until you give birth. Please enjoy this respite. Unless you have another child one day, you'll never get a chance like this again."

He kissed Adrien's forehead and then stood, adjusting his cock beneath his perfect trousers. He pushed a button on the wall, and shades lowered over the skylights, darkening the room while still leaving the soft glow of the blurry green woods outside. "Until later, little one."

And then he was gone, leaving Adrien drowsing on soft sheets, surrounded by a glimmering green forest and the sound of a babbling brook echoing through the solid glass walls.

# Chapter Ten

HEATH HATED TO leave Adrien when he'd only just arrived, flushed with pregnancy hormones and looking so beautiful. He positively ached to strip down with the boy and run his hands over every inch of him before fucking him into senseless submission.

Unfortunately, he had a long-scheduled business meeting with his friend Felix Sanchez he needed to attend first. The very same Felix who had once bragged about having the highest bid for Adrien's first heat and tempted Heath into looking the auction up.

Watching the sunlight shatter against the high-rise glass all around him as his driver took him to Felix's offices in the city, Heath bristled now at that memory. Felix had seen the naked photos of Adrien from the auction site, too. A lot of men had. And while there was nothing shameful about nudity, and Adrien had a beautiful body he should be proud of, right now that body was *Heath's* to protect and care for. He couldn't tolerate the idea of anyone else, except perhaps his favorite old servant Simon, looking at it.

He sighed, tugging at his hair, and then used his fingers to get it back into position. He didn't want to look out of sorts. Felix would ask questions, and questions were something Heath didn't want to answer right now. Not from Felix, and not even from old, devoted Simon.

Speaking of Simon, he had already tutted at Heath for impregnating Adrien at all. And that had been *before* he saw the boy walking through the castle with Heath and had instantly recognized his likeness to Nathan. Heath had been lucky to get out of the castle without Simon boxing his ears for, as he'd put it, 'twisted perversions.'

Heath understood what Simon was on about. He was playing with fire of every kind. Not only was he covering himself in emotional lighter fluid, but he was also potentially torching a decade-long truce between himself and his younger brother, Lidell. A truce achieved because Heath had never managed to procreate.

But now he had.

And there would be hell to pay for that if Lidell had anything to say about it. And he would. Eventually. Lidell had always wanted Clearwater passed to Ned, his auction-born child. A brat with no ambition beyond throwing parties and fucking omegas through heats—and throwing parties centered around fucking desperate omegas outside of heats.

Not that Heath could chide the boy about that. He'd been much the same at Ned's age. What alpha hadn't been? Sex-obsessed pleasure-hounds. But Ned's little group of friends were privileged beyond the telling, and Heath didn't know if Ned would ever grow out of it.

Regardless, Simon had every right to be annoyed with him.

Making a child with Nathan's son was both everything Heath had dreamed of when he'd schemed it and nothing at all like he'd imagined. He hadn't explained to Simon that Adrien had qualities Heath admired for their own sake, and, well, he'd be hard-pressed to even list for Simon what those qualities were, since they mainly involved the very intimate details of how Adrien took being fucked, the sounds he made, and the way he trusted Heath so completely. Something Nathan had never done.

Simon would say he should have gotten to know the boy better before taking this step. But they had four months before the baby came for that, didn't that? That was part and parcel of why omegas were kept separate from the rest of society while they gestated—to promote a bond with the alpha. If the alpha wanted a bond, that was. Many didn't. And he hadn't planned on wanting one, but…

God, he was tired of his own brain. He just wanted to go back to the castle, fuck Adrien, and hold him while they dreamed up names for their baby. Was that too much to ask?

Apparently so. Because the car had arrived at Felix's office building.

The driver opened the car door for him, and he stepped out into the sunset. Heath shaded his eyes before slipping on sunglasses and walking purposefully into the Sanchez Holding Company offices, where he took the elevator up to Felix's private rooms at the top.

Felix was a big, beefy redhead with strong arms and thighs. He looked great in a suit, like he could take a man apart limb by limb while simultaneously making trade deals with the leaders of the fifteen nations of the world. His features were strong and had a patrician air to them, which gave refinement to his big build, and his eyes twinkled with humor and intelligence. He was also, for better or worse, raunchy as all hell.

"So you fucked that kid through his heat, huh?" he asked as soon as Heath walked in. "Paid a fortune to do it, too. Damn, friend, I hope he was worth it." He gripped Heath's hand hard and shook it with a salacious grin on his face.

"He's pregnant," Heath said. He'd kept the news mostly to himself, aside from the doctor he'd put on retainer for Adrien's well-being, and Simon, of course. But he knew if he didn't tell

Felix now, the man would say something that would make Heath put a fist in his face, and that wouldn't be pleasant or profitable for either of them.

"Oh, he wasn't just a pleasure fuck, then?" Felix said, blinking in surprise. "And here I thought you had simply made time for a sensual holiday for two."

"No," Heath said firmly. "I'm making an heir."

"I bet Lidell is thrilled to hear that."

Heath groaned.

"Oh, Lidell doesn't know, does he?" Felix shook his head and cackled, his neck extending back with his glee. "Sweet babies in a basket, Heath! What's going on with you?"

"Business first." Heath shot his cuffs and sat down in the chair opposite Felix's desk. "Fill me in on this investment you're so sold on and convince me to give you the money for it."

Felix smirked but didn't argue. He knew Heath well enough to know that pissing him off now wasn't a good personal or business choice.

The rest of the meeting ran quickly.

"I do appreciate you coming in today," Felix said once the ink was dry on the agreement and Heath had put a large sum of money at his disposal. "As usual, I couldn't do what I do without you."

Heath shrugged. He'd inherited his family's fortune when his parents died, and he had more than he could ever spend. He'd found over the years that money didn't buy happiness, and, if he had his way, he'd spend more time in the woods and less time cutting deals. But he also knew the world around them was going to shit, and if he wanted to make a difference in it, then he needed allies like Felix to fight the good fight, build the good buildings, fund the right work, and organize proper charities. For fuck's sake, he wasn't going to do it himself, now was he?

He stood up, straightened his suit jacket, and said, "I have things to attend to at home. Raincheck on those drinks, friend."

"And by 'things to attend,' do you mean a pregnant omega?" Felix asked.

Heath adjusted his tie. He should have known Felix wasn't going to let the subject go. They'd been friends too long, and Felix knew too much about his family's dramas to not see how Lidell was going to take it and to not wonder what prompted Heath to burn that bridge after all these years.

He cleared his throat, uncertain where to start. Should he tell him all the justifications he'd made up after the fact? Or the truth?

"He was a luscious young man," Felix said. "I was willing to pay a lot to have his heat. I have a few children already, as you know, all of them living with their omega parents because I have no patience for young ones. But if I'd won him, I'd have paid to breed, too. He's handsome and intelligent. I get the urge. I do." Felix tilted his head. "But, Heath, it's not like you."

So the truth, then.

"He's Nathan's son," he said. It came out sounding strangled. He hoped Felix didn't notice. He hadn't meant to give so very much away with so few words.

Felix's eyebrows hit his hairline. "He's what?"

"Nathan's son. His only living descendent. From his first breeding."

Felix stared at Heath and then headed to the liquor cabinet by the wide windows looking out over the city. "No, you're staying for a drink, because this? This is madness."

Heath almost balked, but Felix approached him with a finger and a half of brandy and a worried glimmer in his eye that spoke of true friendship. Heath sighed and took the liquor.

"Your favorite brandy," Felix said.

Heath took a sip.

"Now, sit down here on the sofa," Felix said, guiding Heath toward the area of his office reserved for more casual conversations. "You've impregnated your dead lover's son," Felix said, and Heath had to admit it sounded quite bad when put like that. "Does he know?"

"Who? Nathan? As you stated, he's dead. Of course he doesn't know."

"Don't be purposely obtuse. That won't work with me. You know I meant the son. The omega you won."

Heath sighed, then took another hearty swallow of brandy and raised a brow.

"He doesn't know," Felix concluded, sitting back with wide eyes. "Do you plan to tell him?"

"I don't see why I should."

"Why the hell not?"

"Why would I tell him something like that? It's not important in the scheme of what we're doing together. He'll be gone after the child is born, take the money and…" Heath trailed off. That's what he'd expected Adrien to do. It's what Nathan would have done. But Adrien wasn't Nathan. "There won't be a reason for him to ever know. Even if he chooses to participate in the child's life, he won't be around for long. He wants to be a professor." He shifted uncomfortably.

Felix lifted a brow. "And if you fall for each other during the gestation period?"

"Unlikely."

Felix blew out a low whistle. "I fell for two of my boys' omega parents. They didn't fall for me."

"That's brutal," Heath said, throat tight.

"Yes. Well, what *do* you plan to do?"

Heath took the rest of his glass down in a fast gulp. It wasn't good form, but he didn't care. He needed the burn of alcohol to clear his mind. Or muddy it. He wasn't quite sure which. "I suppose a lot of it is up to him. How well we get on between now and the birth will play a big part. How much of a role he wants in the child's life. How much of a role he wants in mine."

"You? Raising a child alone? No. If you want my advice, let him raise the little booger, and you just leave the castle and the fortune to it. Be done with the whole thing after the heat. If you don't fall in love, all the better."

"I know you don't enjoy fatherhood much, Felix, but I think I'll take to it quite well. He'll be part Nathan, and I always wanted that." And part Adrien, too. He no longer seemed only a Nathan substitute, after all, but his own, sweet, trusting person who made Heath feel all alpha.

"Fine, fine. But you intend to let this boy decide what part he'll play in this child's life without ever telling him why you knocked him up to begin with?" He lifted a brow again. "That seems unfair."

"Adrien is—"

"Ah, yes, Adrien. I'd forgotten his name."

Heath huffed, annoyed by that statement. How anyone could forget anything about Adrien was beyond him. The boy was exquisite, and in bed he made the sweetest, most desperate noises while coming on Heath's knot. He cleared his throat and adjusted his pants.

"What does Simon think of this?"

"He doesn't like it."

"I should say not. The old bugger must be worried that he'll have to change nappies and sing the baby to sleep when this omega goes trotting off with all that money to, as you say, travel the world or finish his schooling."

Heath frowned. "I'll hire a nanny for the child."

"That was Simon's job, wasn't it? Your nanny."

"And now he's my general keeper. He doesn't find it a very fun position."

"At least you aren't throwing ragers with the president's youngest son anymore or keeping omegas on retainer for heat orgies like you did in university."

"I've known you too long, Felix. You have all of my worst secrets on speed dial."

"I also have your best interests at heart. I suppose there's no undoing it now. The boy is well and truly fucked in so many ways, and you'll have to deal with whatever comes." Felix shrugged.

"Yes."

"And what if the baby's not an alpha?"

"Call me new-fangled, but I don't see why an omega or beta can't inherit."

"You wouldn't. But Lidell will. He and Ned will take it to court to get an alpha back in power after you're gone."

"If Lidell outlives me, perhaps he would. But Ned is too lazy. He'll take whatever money is offered and run. Besides, we'll fight those battles as they come." Heath nodded firmly. That was the ticket. Take everything one step at a time. Don't overthink anything. Nothing was certain yet.

Felix shook his head and downed the last of his drink. Then he stood and said, "Well, don't let me delay you further. I'm sure your handsome omega is at home right now just aching from all those sweet pregnancy hormones for a good, long, fu—"

"Don't," Heath said sharply. "Don't talk about him like he's a common whore."

Felix zipped his lips, but his eyes flew wide. "Good God, you're in over your head," he said as he showed Heath out. "Half in love already. He's not Nathan, you know."

Heath shook Felix's hand as he opened the office door. "He isn't. And somehow I find him all the more appealing because of that."

On the drive home, anticipation thrummed in him. He thought over Adrien's arrival earlier in the day and the eager way the boy had stripped for him and gone to his knees. He supposed they should have talked a bit more about the expectations between them, but he'd been overwhelmed with protectiveness and then lust.

It struck him as strange that Adrien knew so little of what to expect from pregnancy, but he seemed to recall Nathan telling him that the man with kind eyes, the one who'd bought his breeding and with whom Nathan had left his son, had been a religious sort. Adrien had confirmed as much in what he'd said about it all. Many religious sects were incredibly backward in their ideas of omega rights.

Regardless, it thrilled some dark, possessive part of him to know that he would be the one to teach Adrien. It was the same part of him that had been thrilled to take Adrien's virginity, his first heat, and to breed him, too. In some ways, Adrien already felt more *his* than Nathan ever had.

# Chapter Eleven

ADRIEN WOKE UP from his nap hungry and a little disoriented. The sun had gone down and the glass-walled room, which had seemed almost like a fairytale when he could see into the green, leafy forest, now seemed somewhat threatening and gloomy.

He was a little cold, too.

He put on his glasses, relieved by the room coming into focus. His clothes were still where he'd left them on the floor, but Heath had told him not to wear them. Would he really care? He wouldn't want Adrien to be chilly, would he? That probably wasn't the best for the baby. He might catch a cold. Or was that just an old tale?

He got out of the fluffy bed, found his glasses, and pulled on his jeans and T-shirt. Sometime during his nap, someone had come into the room with his luggage, and that felt a little creepy. He glanced around, noting the door to the hallway was shut, though there were human sounds coming from outside it. He hurriedly went through his things until he found a soft, warm hoodie and pulled it on.

Then, still unnerved by the growing darkness of the forest and the creaking of the swaying trees outside, and driven by the gnawing in his stomach, he cautiously opened the door and stepped out into the creamy, concrete hallway. The light shafting in from the skylights above was an amber color now, and some electric lights had been turned on in various corners of the hallway.

He followed the sounds of cooking and the scent of something delicious until he stepped into a wide, open area that housed a very comfortable-looking living room and a big kitchen. There was a circular window encompassing one full end of the room and which looked out onto a spacious flower garden and a gazebo near a bridge that passed over the brook. There were even some twinkling lights hung in the ornamental trees, and that, for some reason, surprised Adrien more than almost anything else all day. It seemed such a twee choice for a gruff alpha like Heath.

"Hello!" a cheery voice called from within a pantry built into the thick wall of concrete. A balding, gray-laced head, sporting merry twinkling eyes and a happy smile peeked out from the pantry door. "I'm Simon, and you must be Adrien."

Adrien wrapped his arms around himself, still a little cold, and cleared his throat. "Hi."

"Yes, hi," Simon said, almost laughing. He stepped out of the pantry wearing an old-fashioned butler's uniform, which made Adrien blink as well. "You're cold, I take it? I told him that we'd need to put heaters in that room, but he thought the pregnancy hormones might make you too hot." Simon tutted. "I'm always right, you know. And you can tell him I said that."

Adrien smiled timidly, shoving his glasses up the bridge of his nose. "I am cold, yes. And hungry."

Simon swung open the refrigerator door and pulled out a tray. "I've got you covered, lovey. Have a seat here at the counter. Let's fill you up. Can't have you or the baby going hungry while you wait for dinner."

"Oh." Adrien walked toward the counter that separated the living area from the kitchen. He sat on a stool. "If I eat all this, I'll be too full for dinner."

"That's what you say now! But there's no rush. You have all evening to eat. Heath wants you fattened up. He's worried that you're too thin."

Adrien looked down at himself, noting how the hoodie and jeans hung on him. "I've been sick lately."

"From the baby," Simon said knowingly. "Being here with Heath will fix that. There are soothing properties in the… Ah, well…" He flushed and waved vaguely. "And the pheromones, too. You'll be more comfortable now that you're with us," he finished up with a happy smile.

Adrien accepted the glass of water Simon pressed into his hand, as well as a handful of supplements.

"Vitamins. Everything the doctor ordered to grow a strong child."

He swallowed them, feeling oddly childlike, and memories of the time he'd been sick with a terrible illness swept over him. He remembered his father praying by his side, refusing the doctor's orders for medications, until, finally, so frightened that Adrien might die, he'd given in and let the doctor give him the handful of pills that helped him get better.

In a way, his father's worst fears about the medicine came true. His return to health at the hands of science had been part of why Adrien eventually stepped away from the religion his father had adhered to so blindly. His youthful infatuation with the handsome doctor might have also inspired him to consider leaving their little town, but it was the magazine the doctor left behind with photos of art from around the fifteen countries of the world that had inspired him to go to college.

Something about Simon reminded him of that sickness. The caretaking, perhaps. The scent of roasting vegetables, maybe.

"When will Heath be back?" he asked after he no longer felt like he would fall off the stool in hunger.

Simon smiled again, shoving a big casserole of some kind into the oven. Adrien's mouth watered, even though he'd just consumed half the plate of cheese, meat, and bread that Simon had set out in front of him. "He'll be here soon, I imagine." He glanced toward another big steel-and-wood clock. It somehow looked more appropriate in this room, built into the earth beneath the castle as it was. "He hated to leave you, but he'd agreed to this appointment before he knew you were coming today."

"It's all right," Adrien said. His cheeks heated as he remembered the way they'd spent the very short time they'd had together before Heath had left.

"Let me light a fire in the big oven down the hall. It will warm the walls." He smiled again. "I'll also call for some small heaters to be put in your room. I'll be right back."

Once he was alone, Adrien stood up and explored the space. It didn't look anything like the part of the castle he'd followed Heath through to get here. It was like a rabbit's den: cozy, nesty, warm. And the light from the sunset cast a glow against the creamy walls, making Adrien relax. His breathing came in steady, soothing waves.

He ran his fingers over the low, soft couches and the similarly comfortable-looking chairs. There were throw pillows, some big enough to be chairs in their own right, a comfortable chaise, and several ottomans. Additional books lined one wall of this room, but there was no entertainment center that he could see. Fluffy rugs felt nice under his bare feet, and he sighed as the heat from the oven, wherever it was located, kicked in and the room seemed to embrace him with warmth breathing through invisible vents and the walls themselves.

"Yes, make yourself at home," Simon said, returning to find Adrien testing out the couch. "And if those clothes start to bother you as the room warms up, take them off. Heath will be worried to see you dressed."

Adrien blushed. "You mean I should…? With you here? I don't know. It's, ah, that's…"

Simon waved a hand dismissively. "Do what makes you comfortable, lovey. As the pregnancy progresses, your skin will become more and more sensitive. Just know that I've seen many a naked man in my life and find them, in general, highly unremarkable. You are completely safe with me."

Adrien mumbled some vague response and grabbed a book from the shelf, feigning extreme interest in it to prevent any more talking or thinking about his body or nudity. Or his skin being sensitive. Or his body changing.

He still hadn't allowed himself to think much about any of that.

"I apologize that I'm so late."

Adrien's heart kicked, and he looked up to find Heath walking toward him from the door that led out to the hall. He wore his suit still and looked more handsome than the last time Adrien had seen him, though he still missed the beard.

"I see you've met Simon."

Adrien started to stand up, but Heath put out a hand to stop him. "Stay comfortable." He frowned. "You're wearing clothes."

"I was cold."

"I told you," Simon said from the kitchen where he bent to pull the casserole from the oven again. The cheesy, delicious scent made Adrien's mouth explode with saliva and his stomach, which had seemed so full only moments ago, groan with hunger.

"Did you start the big oven and have heaters put into his room?"

"I did."

"Yes. Thank you. I can feel that it's warming up in here."

Heath tugged at his tie and tossed his coat onto a nearby chair. He rubbed his hands through his hair, messing up the perfectly coiffed darkness, leaving it a handsome, shaggy mess that fell into his gray eyes. He removed his cufflinks and folded his shirtsleeves up his forearms, revealing the hairy, ropey muscles that Adrien suddenly remembered gripping in the throes of heat.

He flushed, his cock growing thick in his jeans and his mouth pulsing with more saliva. He glanced toward Simon, embarrassed to be aroused in front of him.

"Take your clothes off," Heath said. "Your body needs to breathe."

"I can breathe with my clothes on," Adrien said, putting his chin up. He wasn't going to be naked and hard in front of Simon, no matter what Heath said.

Heath regarded him thoughtfully, but clearly decided not to push the issue. For some reason, Adrien had the impression that the discussion wasn't over, so much as shelved for another time.

"The food is prepared, the heating issue is resolved, and I believe the two of you should be alone." Simon straightened his uniform and put up his chin, his jowls wobbling a little in a friendly sort of way. Something about Simon was so comforting to Adrien that he almost hated to see him go, but at the same time, if Heath was going to insist that he get naked—and the other things Adrien wanted to do *did* require nakedness—then he supposed it was best if Simon left.

"I'll be back in the morning to make his breakfast, see to the laundry you'll no doubt make"—this was said in a cheeky way that made Adrien squirm, but didn't imply any discomfort on Simon's part,—"and, of course, make sure that he gets some fresh air and sunshine while you're at the office. In the meantime, I think I'll go home, read a few chapters of a nice spy novel, and toddle off to bed."

Heath tore his gaze from Adrien and smiled softly at Simon. It was, perhaps, the first time Adrien had seen this sort of expression on Heath's face. He seemed fond, almost like how a child looked at a doting parent. "Sleep well, old man."

"I'll sleep however I damn well please," Simon said haughtily. "There are some things in life you can't control, *young* man." Then he left without a backward glance, while Heath gazed after him, chuckling under his breath.

"So that's Simon," Heath said when he finally turned his attention back to Adrien. "He was my nurse, then my tutor, and then my only real family after my parents died." His lips twisted. "Well, if I don't count my brother, and I don't."

"You have a brother?"

"Younger. We don't get along. Regardless, Simon runs my household now. Though, until you leave, his main duty will be you."

"I don't need anyone to take care of me," Adrien said. "I've lived on my own for a long time now."

"Right. Since your father's death."

Adrien nodded, his throat going dry. Something about the way Heath said 'your father' felt strange, and he couldn't put his finger on why. "I've lived in the dorms at the university. I can manage."

"The dorms. I see. I believe the dorms provide you with meals and janitorial services. Think of Simon as a friendlier, more personal version of that."

Adrien didn't think he could treat the old man the way he'd treated the cafeteria workers and janitors at the university. To be truthful, he'd barely given them a second glance or ever offered them a thanks. He frowned. It was possible he was a complete dick.

"He's nice," Adrien said softly. His stomach growled again as the scent of the casserole Simon had made drifted through the room to him. "This place is…nice."

Heath laughed, short and curt. "It's the only nice part of this ridiculous castle. And it should be. I made it myself. Or hired it to be made, rather. I'm afraid that aside from splitting logs for the fireplace at the heat cabin, I don't do much with my hands."

Adrien chewed on his lower lip, his eyes drifting to the casserole dish. He wondered if he could suggest that they eat now, or if he should let Heath do that. He wasn't a guest, yet this wasn't his home. He didn't quite know the protocol. He licked his lips, and his stomach grumbled again.

Heath heard it this time. "Get over to the table. You need to eat."

Adrien obeyed, like he always did when Heath spoke in commands. It was odd, though, for a man in a beautiful suit to serve him heaping servings of a cheesy chicken casserole, and fetch water for him, and offer him a glass of fizzing juice that was said to calm pregnancy stomach.

"There," Heath said, sitting beside him with a much smaller helping of food. "Eat as much as you can. You're skin and bones."

Adrien didn't say anything to that, hurrying to get the delicious food into his mouth instead. As he ate, he felt Heath's eyes on him, and he was grateful when Heath stood up and turned on some soft music that drifted from hidden speakers all over the room.

"Tell me about your father," Heath said suddenly. "And your omega parent, whatever you know about him."

Adrien frowned. "My father was a kind man. Stern, perhaps, but loving. He was religious and sent me to a religion-based school in our small town. I decided to go to college though, and, had he lived long enough, no doubt that news would have broken his heart. I don't know if I could have done that to him, actually. But he died." Adrien poked at his cheesy casserole with his fork and then admitted, "I miss him."

"I see."

Adrien cocked his head. "Why do you want to know?"

"Curiosity. We're making a child together. I wondered about your experience and expectations of parenthood."

"Oh." Adrien ate some more food and then said, "I never knew the omega who birthed me. My father said he was smart and funny. I apparently look quite a lot like him."

Heath made a small noise, but said nothing, tucking into his food like he suddenly remembered it was there.

"They only spent the heat and pregnancy together. So, in the scheme of life, my father didn't know him long. But he said he was irreverent and a terrible heathen. But he must have been charming, too, because my father always said that like it was a compliment, and he would never have said it like that for anyone else. Not even me."

Heath met his eyes, opened his mouth as if he was about to say something, and then closed it again.

"What about you?" Adrien asked. "What were your parents like? Did you know them both?"

"I did. They were a married couple. Which is more and more unusual these days, I know. Due to omega freedom rights."

Adrien's brow went up. "Do you not agree with the new legislature?"

"I absolutely agree with it," Heath said sternly. "But the point in fact is that my father and omega parent would not have stayed together in today's world. Of that I feel quite sure. My da—that's what my omega parent liked to be called—was always complaining about the things he'd missed out on being married so young. And they fought."

Adrien listened carefully as he ate, surprised by the way Heath spoke so casually now. In the heat cabin, he'd been gruff, rough, and often silent. They'd fucked and grunted, and he'd ordered Adrien around, but he'd rarely offered up any conversation at all. This seemed like a whole new man. Until he focused his gray eyes on Adrien and commanded, "Eat."

"I am!" Adrien exclaimed, annoyed. "I have to let it digest. My stomach is stuffed, but I'm still hungry."

Heath frowned. "They should have sent you earlier."

"They sent me as soon as the pregnancy was confirmed."

Heath glared at that. "They should have just let you stay with me after the heat. Then you'd have never been sick at all."

Adrien sighed and pushed the food around on his plate. "I'm full. I'm sorry."

Heath relented then. "You can't be expected to return to full health in a few hours. I'll take it away. You can eat more later. The pantry and refrigerator are stocked with healthy foods for you."

"And if I want cake?" Adrien challenged, a vague sense of panic settling over him as the night grew dark out the wide, round window and a hint of claustrophobia began to set in.

"Then you'll have cake," Heath said with equal challenge. "Did you expect something different? You aren't a prisoner."

"Are you sure about that?" Adrien asked. "I feel trapped."

Heath stared at him, a wounded look flashing over his face. "If these quarters aren't suitable then—"

"No!" The idea of being housed in the cold, baroque areas of the castle that he'd walked through to reach this warm nest was horrifying. Beyond that, it simply wasn't what he meant. "I'm happy with these rooms, but…am I allowed to leave? To talk to friends? Do I just sit here and read books alone until I pop this baby out of my ass?" He hadn't meant to be crude, but Heath's expression of surprised amusement made it worth it. "What's my life going to be like? Like, okay, I have this baby inside me, and it's strange, but I can't escape him. That's odd, isn't it? Can you imagine what that's like?"

Heath took Adrien's plate to the kitchen, washed it in the sink, and then left it aside. "I can't," he said slowly. "And I don't know what your life will look like here. I do know that omegas are kept away from the public for the length of the pregnancy for their safety, comfort, and pleasure. I'll do everything I can to make your stay here pleasurable, Adrien." His voice went husky, and Adrien's cock liked that.

"I can call my friends?"

"You have a cell phone, don't you? If not, I'll get you one."

Adrien did, but he hadn't even looked at it since he arrived. It'd been stuffed in the bottom of his bag. Because, truth be told, aside from Lance, he wasn't sure anyone would miss him. His professors and colleagues had wished him well, but none of them were likely to want to check in. His co-researchers barely spoke to him outside of their work on the project. And his father was long gone.

A sudden, painful loneliness gripped him, and his throat went embarrassingly tight as his eyes filled with tears. He shoved his glasses on top of his head and wiped ferociously at his eyes. He would not cry. And over what?

Over how completely confused he was and how uncertain the future seemed? Over how he had no one in his life to even worry about him while he was gone living with a stranger and birthing a child?

Wow, he was pathetic, and he hadn't even known it.

"What?" Heath said, coming closer, every inch of him looking like a protective alpha, ready to slaughter whatever or whomever was upsetting his pregnant omega.

Oh, God, *he* was this man's omega.

He was stuffed with this strange man's child, and he was trapped here in this nest for the next four months. He breathed roughly, trying to get a good lungful, but the room started to spin around him.

"Adrien?"

He stood up from the table and tried to speak, desperate for some fresh air, but the spots in his vision swirled faster and darker, and then it was all very black.

# Chapter Twelve

HEATH CAUGHT ADRIEN as he fell, eyes rolled back in his head and his body going suddenly pale and limp. He patted Adrien's cheeks, relieved when he opened his eyes and muttered, "Need some air."

They'd just turned on the heat because Adrien was too cold, for God's sake, but who was he to argue with a pregnant omega? He lifted Adrien easily—he really had lost weight since the heat cabin—and opened the door leading out to the walled garden. The twinkling lights Simon had insisted on putting on the fruit trees gave enough light to see by, along with the full moon. Adrien's color was returning. He sat down on the closest bench by a flowering rosebush and cradled Adrien against his chest.

"Did I pass out?" Adrien asked, his breath a puff against Heath's throat.

"Yes."

"I got too hot."

"We can turn the heat down. The oven can be adjusted and the heat reduced."

"No. I'll be too cold."

Heath huffed a laugh. "Which is it?"

Adrien struggled out of his lap, wiping a hand over his mouth and pulling at his clothes. "I don't know. I felt like I couldn't breathe."

"Do you feel better now?" He kept his hand on Adrien's

back, but he didn't move it in the stroking, soothing manner Simon had used when he'd been sick as a child. He simply held it there, steady and sure, and tried to judge if Adrien was going to bolt, or cry, or scream. He felt a building tension in the air alongside the sweet scent of the roses.

"I don't have anyone who cares where I am," Adrien said finally, taking in shaky, slow breaths. The cool night air was making his cheeks go pink. His glasses had slipped again, and Adrien straightened them.

"I'm not going to hurt you," Heath said, hearing the need for reassurance in his omega's voice. "You're safe here. I promise."

"I know. Maybe I'm too safe." He smiled with a hint of embarrassment. "I mean, I feel caged in."

"What will help with that? You have your phone. There's this garden always at your disposal. If you want to go out on the town, I can take you. Or the driver can take you. At least until you start to show, and then I think you'll be far too uncomfortable to want to leave."

"You keep saying that." Adrien tugged at his jeans again, adjusting the fall of his hoodie.

"It's just the facts. I have some books inside about pregnancy and birth. You'll read them," he said, pushing command into his tone, knowing that Adrien would respond to it the same way he had from the moment they'd met.

"What if they scare me more?"

"It's better to know what to expect than to be taken unawares."

"I guess." Adrien tugged on his hoodie again. "This is… It's…" He pulled at the bottom of it, and then finally huffed, tugging it off. His skin prickled with goosebumps in the night air, and his nipples hardened into pink nubs. "There," he sighed. "I can breathe."

Heath said nothing. He only looked at Adrien with meaning in his eyes, and finally Adrien's head bowed.

"Oh."

"Yes."

"That's what you've been telling me about the clothes."

Heath put a hand on Adrien's back, his muscles leaping underneath his skimming touch. "It will only get worse. After the baby comes, once you're past the critical first few days, clothes won't bother you so much, and you'll probably look forward to wearing them again."

Some omegas didn't like it, though, and continued to go nude at home for the rest of their lives. He didn't think he'd tell Adrien that. Not yet. He seemed so shaken already. Heath wondered what Adrien would think of the other changes his body would undergo—the widening of his hips and the lactation, just to start.

"Here's what we're going to do," Heath said calmly, keeping his voice low. He could sense Adrien's reaction to that timbre in the way his muscles relaxed beneath Heath's hands and the small shudder of arousal that went through him. "We're going back inside, and I'm going to fuck you. That will calm you down. Afterward, we're going to rest together and start reading one of the pregnancy books. I'll help you through whatever feelings come up about that."

Adrien shoved his glasses up the bridge of his nose, looking around at the rose garden in the darkness. Their scent rose around them with every small breeze. "Do you like roses?"

"Yes."

"I do, too," he said quietly.

Heath turned to the bush next to them, which he knew was full of fat pink roses with an orangey tip. They smelled sweet, but also spicy, and he carefully tugged a blossom free and handed it to

Adrien, who sniffed it and smiled.

Heath placed his hand on Adrien's neck. "The garden is full of them. Tomorrow morning, after breakfast, we'll walk out here."

"Naked?" Adrien asked in a small voice.

"It's up to you. I'll be clothed."

"That hardly seems fair."

"It's the nature of things," Heath stated. "But we'll be naked together in your room."

"I've never been naked outside," Adrien said, hiding his face by sniffing the rose again. "Or in front of anyone but you. Aside from when I had the pictures made for the auction."

"Not even in the dorm showers?"

"We have stalls."

Heath had lived in those dorms as well, having attended the university twenty years earlier. The difference was, he'd been a randy alpha, and he'd brought plenty of willing omegas up to play. He frowned at his memories. He'd been an awful, entitled asshole back then.

"I wore a robe in the hallway. My father always said modesty was important in an omega," Adrien said quickly, as though to prove he wasn't acting without reason.

"Of course," Heath said. He threaded his fingers into Adrien's blond hair, a shimmer of rage under his skin at the thought that any alpha might have ever treated Adrien as casually as he'd treated omegas in college. He pushed it down by reminding himself that was not the case and that Adrien had never been touched by anyone but himself.

He really shouldn't feel so chuffed about that. But he did.

"I don't want to be naked in front of Simon," Adrien said. "Or anyone else."

"I see."

Adrien met his gaze again, his eyes bright with determination. "Who do you expect me to be naked in front of exactly? Your servants? Your *friends*?"

Adrien really had led a sheltered life if nudity was such a problem for him. Most city omegas were content to be naked in their homes. It usually meant they were more likely to get laid, and, if they were lucky, find a mate to build a life with. But religious families were different. Clearly, Nathan hadn't cared at all that his baby was going to be raised by a conservative, sex-shaming man of faith.

*He had such kind eyes.* He heard Nathan's voice in his head, a little dazed with remembered bliss even all those years later. *I left the baby with him because I didn't want to raise him. And, oh, Heath, I know he's in good hands. His father had such kind eyes.*

Leave it to Nathan to think of little but himself. Typically infuriating and selfish. And yet Heath had loved him anyway. Desperately loved him. Maybe he'd been a fool all these years ago to hope that Nathan had loved him back. Still, if he hadn't loved Nathan, then he wouldn't be sitting here with Adrien, who was pregnant with his child. God, what an impulsive, beautiful, wonderful, probably stupid idea that had been. Now he just needed to calm Adrien down, keep him safe, and hope that…

Hope that what?

He shut down that train of thought. It was far too early for any hopes other than a healthy baby.

"You don't have to be naked in front of anyone. I'll find a robe for you, something light that hopefully won't bother your skin, and you can wear that when Simon is around. How many people you see while you're here is up to you. As for whether I want you to be naked with my friends? That's nonnegotiable. You will never be naked in front of my friends. Or any alphas, period."

Adrien swallowed hard. "Never?"

"So long as you're with me, I will be the only alpha to see your flesh."

Adrien nodded. "I'm nervous."

"You were nervous in the cabin, and that turned out all right."

Adrien touched his stomach, shivering in the cool night air. He sniffed the rose again. "Can people see us?" He glanced back over his shoulder at the castle behind them. "From inside?"

"The only people inside are servants—all betas. But, no, this garden is built at an angle that makes it always just out of view from any windows."

Adrien frowned. "But why?"

"Because I like my privacy."

"You don't get enough of that in this giant house?"

"This part was built on when I first decided years ago to court an omega and start a family. I intended it for my omega's nest to gestate and birth our child. It simply took longer than I expected to find that omega."

Adrien sniffed the rose again. "You didn't court me. You bought me. At an auction."

Heath hesitated, but his next words felt right. The heat crush had worn off, and in its place was his urgent desire to soothe his pregnant omega, and a small vibrant thread of hope that was sewing itself into his ridiculous, open heart. "Then allow me to court you now."

"By fucking me?"

"Yes. By taking care of you." He touched Adrien's chin, bringing his gaze up. "By teaching you how to get through this."

"All right," Adrien agreed. "I guess I don't have a choice."

"Do you want a choice?"

Adrien chewed on his bottom lip and then met Heath's eyes,

heat blazing there, and a bit of sheepishness, too. “No.”

“Then get inside. I’m going to fuck you.”

“Then we’ll read?”

“Yes. Then we’ll read.”

# Chapter Thirteen

ADRIEN DIDN'T KNOW why he was so surprised that every word out of Heath's mouth relaxed him, or that the scent of him sitting beside him on the bench left him feeling open and agreeable. But it did.

"Am I supposed to be so willing?" he whispered as Heath led him by the hand back into the cozy living area of the nest. He didn't let go of Heath's hand, following him as he used dimmers on the lights to make the room not so bright. Then he let him lead him to the couch and readily sat beside him.

"Pheromones," Heath said. "Like with heat, but different. You're pregnant with my child. Your brain recognizes that based on my pheromones. That calms you. But fucking you will calm you more."

"How do you know these things?"

"They teach alphas all of this. And remember there was an omega I bred who miscarried. But, in the early stages, before it all came to naught, he went through similar feelings." Heath sounded ashamed to bring that up.

"Oh." Adrien felt a nasty spot of jealousy grow on his heart. What was that about? The other omega was long gone. "You built this place for him?"

"No, I had another omega in mind." He frowned.

Adrien studied him, trying to decide if he wanted to ask or if his jealousy would make it too hard.

"I could tell you about him," Heath offered, though he didn't seem to really want to discuss it. "The omega I had in mind."

In a flash, Adrien decided. "No. I don't want to hear about another omega that you wanted to make a child with." He touched his stomach, thinking of the life within. "Let me pretend that you had this all built for me." He smiled self-consciously. "It's easier that way. I won't be here forever, and it's a nice fantasy."

"You're a sweet man." Heath pulled Adrien close. "I want to feel your skin."

"Yes, okay," Adrien agreed. Then he flushed hot all over. "These jeans!" he complained, tugging at the waist of them.

"Take them off."

"I, uh, haven't showered," Adrien said softly, tugging the jeans and underwear down and kicking them off. He realized he had bare feet and had been out in the garden shoeless. Where was his mind? "I should shower."

"No. I like the way you smell." Heath smiled, running his hands over Adrien's chest and down to his waist. He bent in close and sniffed at Adrien's neck, the breath tickling him and making Adrien giggle. Heath removed Adrien's glasses and put them on the arm of the couch.

"You like the way I smell, too," Heath said, unbuttoning his shirt and tossing it aside. He wore a V-necked undershirt beneath, and he tugged it over his head. Then he reached around for Adrien's nape and hauled him in. "Sniff," he ordered, holding Adrien's face to his armpit. "Take a good, deep breath."

As Adrien did, the sweaty scent of Heath's pits filling his nostrils, he felt tension leach out of him.

"There," Heath murmured.

"You're more open here," Adrien said when Heath released him and began to undress. "In the cabin, you were more closed off."

Heath paused, bent over taking off his shoes and socks. He shoved them behind the giant ottoman serving as a kind of coffee table and then worked on undoing his pants. "I wasn't sure if the pregnancy would take." He sounded gruff now, like his throat was tight, and Adrien wondered if he was holding something back. "I didn't want to feel..." He cleared his throat. "I wasn't sure if an investment would be necessary. Now I know. You're mine for the next few months. And I'm yours."

He stripped naked as Adrien sat on the sofa and watched. Adrien's cock throbbed and rose up against his stomach, and he shuddered in anticipation as Heath revealed his hairy chest, his buttocks, and the muscular thighs that Adrien remembered holding him open, while the giant cock, rising from a thick riot of pubes, had plowed into him.

He felt himself leak slick. Not nearly as much as during heat, but enough. His nipples tingled and his balls rushed with omega fluid—devoid of sperm, but thick and pleasurable to spurt at orgasm. He might be ignorant of a lot of things about being pregnant, but he knew that omegas were sterile.

Heath sat down beside him and spread his legs. "C'mon, little one. Ride me," he ordered.

Adrien's thighs shook as he scrambled to obey. He straddled Heath's hips and held himself upright with two hands on Heath's shoulders. He gazed down at Heath's face, staring into his gray eyes as he slowly lowered down until the tip of Heath's huge cock pushed against his hole.

"Slick enough?" Heath asked. "Or should I finger you?"

The question alone made Adrien convulse and release another rush of slick, so that it slipped down his thighs and coated Heath's cock.

"Slick enough, then." Heath's gravelly rasp sent shivers up

and down Adrien's spine.

Adrien threw his head back, a low moan escaping him, as Heath shoved in. Slow and hard, long and deep, until Adrien sat against his thighs with Heath's cock buried balls deep. Adrien shifted experimentally and shuddered all over, his cock leaking pre-cum against his belly and smearing Heath's, too.

Heath wrapped his arms around Adrien, bringing him in tight, and then pulled his head down to rest on his shoulder. "Now, just breathe here," Heath murmured, holding Adrien close. "Feel me inside you."

"This won't hurt the baby?" Adrien asked, feeling how very deep Heath had plunged into him. He could feel the tip of Heath's cock against the mouth of his womb.

"Fucking is good for him," Heath said. "It bonds us. And it's good for you. It relaxes your passage and hole. It'll make it easier when it's time for the birth."

Adrien didn't want to think about giving birth right then. He wanted to lose himself in the pleasure of having Heath's thickness push hard against his prostate and slick glands.

"Now," Heath said, "ride me."

Adrien tentatively moved his hips and when Heath growled pleasurably, he moved them faster. He started with a circular motion, but soon that wasn't enough. He bounced in Heath's lap, gripping his shoulders but keeping his face tucked close to Heath's neck, breathing in his delicious, masculine scent, as he fucked himself relentlessly on Heath's cock.

"That's it, little one," Heath gritted out. "Hungry little slut. Take my cock."

Adrien shuddered. He'd never imagined being called filthy names until the heat cabin when Heath had called him a slut. But he found he liked it. It made him feel dirty, somehow, in a good way. A way that his father wouldn't have understood—a way that made Adrien's cock throb harder and his ass spasm convulsively around Heath's big dick.

"I love it," Adrien muttered, pressing his face tighter against Heath's neck. "Feels so good."

"Mm." Heath rubbed his back and then just held on to him as Adrien did all the work.

Soon he was slick with sweat and aching all over. His cock dripped with pre-cum, smearing it all over Heath's muscled stomach, and his nipples tingled from rubbing relentlessly against Heath's hairy chest. He wanted to come without touching his cock, like he had in the heat cabin, but he couldn't seem to get there.

Slick rushed out of him, until their thighs were wet and every slap of their skin stung. He moaned and clung to Heath harder, his body aching for orgasm, his skin feeling stretched too thin as he strove for it.

"Oh fuck," Heath groaned, suddenly clutching Adrien's ass and stilling his movements before fucking up into him roughly, wildly, holding Adrien tight enough that his cock rubbed against Heath's muscles hard. He whispered, "Come for me, Adrien. Now. Come now."

Adrien clenched Heath's shoulders, pushed down with his ass, and felt himself open wide for Heath's reckless plunging. His prostate lit up, a jolt like electricity up his spine, and he snapped his head up, eyes rolling back, as he found his shocking climax and pulsed into it.

"Fuck!" Heath yelled, and he kissed Adrien's chest and throat, fucking him as the scent of Adrien's spunk rose between them, slicking the channel of their bodies even more. "Good boy," he moaned and ducked to kiss Adrien's left nipple. "That's my good boy."

Then Heath shuddered all over, his cock growing harder in

Adrien's clinging channel, and he shot hard into Adrien's quivering body. He felt Heath's cum, hot and hard, jetting inside him, and he squeezed his asshole tight around Heath's still-moving cock, desperate to keep his cum inside.

"That's it, yes," Heath murmured, shaking hard, his hips jerking uncontrollably. "Oh, fuck, that's hot."

Adrien's cock shot off again between them, and Heath cried out, another volley of cum blasting into Adrien's ass.

And then they calmed.

Adrien collapsed, sweaty and so tired, his cheek against Heath's shoulder. And Heath held him close, his head back against the couch, and his breath coming in heaving pants. Adrien was no better. He panted against Heath's sweaty skin.

"Feel better?" Heath asked.

Adrien laughed, the absurdity of having just been fucked to calmness floating through his mind. And yet it had worked. He was too satisfied now to care much about what was going to happen next, or what it meant that he wouldn't want to wear clothes, or what it meant to have the heir to this crazy castle and fortune growing in his belly.

He could just relax on Heath's strong body, feeling his cock still twitching inside, and rest. It was okay to rest here. He was allowed.

He could learn to love this sense of safety and this full feeling of being plugged by Heath's cock. He could learn to love a lot of things if it meant he could get fucked like this and then be held so tight after. He felt, for the first time since his father's death, cherished and loved.

"WHERE DO YOU sleep?"

Heath was startled from the blissful reverie he'd been drifting in, stuffed deep into his omega's body and scenting his relaxed pleasure as he cuddled on the couch in Heath's arms. "What's that?" he asked again, dragging his attention away from the fluorescent sensation of happiness glowing in his cells.

"Do you sleep with me or…?"

Heath picked up Adrien's glasses from their safe spot on the arm of the couch and deposited them carefully on his face again. "I usually sleep in a room in the main section of the house." He phrased it with deliberate vagueness, because he didn't want to explain that it was the room Nathan had chosen when he moved in, and which Heath had never left. In fact, he was starting to think that he never wanted to explain to Adrien about Nathan at all. It was all better left in the past. "Why?"

"Oh." Adrien tensed against him. "That's fine."

"Do you want me to sleep with you?" Heath asked, surprised that he hadn't thought of it himself. His omega would need protection in the dark of the night.

"It's just that…" Adrien shivered against him, his asshole milking Heath's cock lightly. "The bedroom is great in the daytime, but at night…the forest is…"

"I'll stay with you. Protect you from the park's deer," Heath teased. But in reality, he was pleased. If Adrien wanted him in his bed already, then they were bonding well. Perhaps he wouldn't be like Nathan and want to leave the child behind. Perhaps, he'd stay and…

Too soon. He shut off that line of thought.

"I don't like that I can't see if anyone is out there. Watching me."

"The security for my property is incredibly tight, but there are window screens that you can pull down." He almost regretted being honest about that. What if Adrien didn't want him to stay now?

"There are?"

"I'll show you."

"Okay." But the stiffness in Adrien's body returned. Heath could feel it in the tension around his cock and the tightness of the muscles of Adrien's back.

"What?"

"If we pull the screens down, I'm sure I won't be scared anymore. You won't have to stay then."

"But you want me to stay anyway?" Heath asked, sensing the truth in his body.

Adrien nodded.

"I want to stay with you, too," Heath admitted. "In fact, I'd stay with you exactly like this forever if I could." He pushed his cock up into Adrien a bit deeper.

Adrien smiled, but he said, "Simon would probably complain if he had to feed us while we're stuck together."

Heath chuckled, squeezing Adrien tight, and then he heaved up to standing with his cock still buried deep. Adrien's legs went instinctively around his waist. "Let's go to your bedroom. The books I was telling you about are in there."

With great reluctance, he lifted Adrien off his cock, gratified by the boy's shudder and gasp as his thick dick left him. He didn't put him on his feet, though, enjoying the size difference between them, even if he did think Adrien needed to put on some weight. Heath carried Adrien easily, legs slung over one arm and his back rested against his other. Adrien's arms wrapped around Heath's neck, and he helped support his weight.

"This is a little silly," Adrien said, as they drew closer to his room. "Being carried. I can walk."

"Indulge me," Heath said, inserting that edge of command that turned Adrien to mush. Predictably, Adrien relaxed in his arms and laid his head on Heath's chest, rubbing his cheek against the hair there.

The room was neat except for the messy bed that Adrien hadn't bothered to make when he got up from his nap earlier in the afternoon. Heath put Adrien down in the soft bed, lowered the window screens to block out the admittedly ominous night forest, and turned to the bookshelves. It was warm in the room with the space heaters going, but the windows had let a lot of it leach out, too.

Heath raised a brow, rethinking the whimsy of this glass-walled bedroom. He'd imagined it as romantic for Nathan—because, of course, that was whom he'd built these rooms for. But then Nathan had never wanted to carry a child with him, and, worse, had preferred the rococo rooms above, being a dramatic sort of man. It'd hurt Heath when he'd realized that the nest he'd built as a lure to capture the man of his dreams had been rejected out of hand, along with his wish for a child.

Nathan was charming but coldhearted. Adrien, on the other hand, lacked some of his omega parent's intense charisma but more than eclipsed him in innocence and warmth. Though Heath was loath to declare one better than the other. Omegas were like any other kind of man—different from one to the next, with values and passions that didn't always match the alpha they chose to breed with. It was why omega rights had become so important over the years. And why he had always valued Nathan's unique mind and heart.

But, as he was finding now, perhaps he'd always personally needed someone more like Adrien. Someone who melted into him, opened to him, and trusted him against even his own fears.

"Here it is," Heath said, shaking off his thoughts as he grabbed the book from the shelf. "*Omegas and Pregnancy: What to Expect.* This book contains explanations of heat, pregnancy, and birth, along with important questions to consider for the future of the family," Heath read aloud from the cover. "Fairly comprehensive stuff."

Adrien watched from the bed, wide-eyed behind his glasses and still flushed from the sex they'd shared. "I've always wanted to know more about how our bodies work but was always ashamed to ask," he admitted. "I should have made it more of a priority in university. The omega research books in the library probably had some more detailed options for me to check out. I honestly just didn't want to think about it."

"It's complicated," Heath said. He got into the bed with Adrien, fine-tuned the brightness of the lights in the room, and adjusted the pillows so that he was comfortable.

Adrien curled against his side, easy as could be, like it was where he belonged. Heath's heart squeezed, and he tried to keep himself from thinking along those lines. The questions at the end of the book—they wouldn't reach them for many weeks if they read a few pages a night—might help clarify things for him, but for now he just wanted to enjoy Adrien's scent and touch. To feel his purpose as an alpha fulfilled by the man in his arms and the child he held within.

"'Chapter One, Heat,' " he read aloud, curious if Adrien would protest that he already knew about that, having just gone through it.

But the boy kept quiet, rubbing his cheek against Heath's chest hair and listening as Heath reviewed the subject in depth.

And when Adrien fell asleep in his arms, Heath admitted to himself that he'd be content to spend every evening just like this one for the rest of Adrien's pregnancy. Everything felt right, and so long as he thought about nothing but Adrien, he could dare to let his heart dream.

# Chapter Fourteen

"I THINK YOU'RE going to have to tell him," Simon said, grabbing Heath's arm by the massive front doors of the upstairs castle as he headed out into the midday sun for yet another appointment.

"Let the man gestate in peace," Heath said, jerking his arm away from his oldest friend. "He doesn't deserve to have his pregnancy all twisted up with information about his omega parent. He's happy. Let him enjoy that." Heath paused on the front steps and turned back around.

Simon stood framed by the big doors, arms crossed, and jowls shaking as he gnashed his teeth.

"He is happy, isn't he?" Heath asked. Simon was with Adrien all day. He'd know better than Heath who only saw him in the evenings after work and appointments were knocked off his calendar.

"I wasn't speaking of Adrien, but, yes, he's happy. Though you should tell him, too."

Heath walked back up the stairs and tugged Simon into the cool shadows of the opulent entryway. "What are you going on about then?"

"Your brother. You should tell him about the baby."

Heath rubbed his forehead. "I don't see why I should."

"Because he deserves to know that his and Ned's fortunes have changed."

Heath snorted. "Don't think I'm not perfectly aware of why you want me to tell Lidell. It would make things easier at home for you."

"That it would. Is my comfort in my home life so insignificant to you that you'd begrudge me that?"

Heath stared into Simon's loving eyes. He knew the old man was using his affection to manipulate certain outcomes, but he couldn't truly blame him for it. "I have absolutely no desire to endure Lidell's tantrum when the child isn't even born yet. Adrien is still very early in the pregnancy. He isn't even past the point where I lost the last one."

"That's a fair observation," Simon conceded. "But you know this pregnancy seems to be going much better than that one did. You're bonding well, and Adrien's relaxed and eating nicely. Nathan isn't here to put a strain on him."

Heath felt the muscle in his jaw twitch, and he took an extra moment before replying, "It was never Nathan's fault that my first child was lost."

"Wasn't it?"

"No!" Heath barked.

Simon shrugged. "It was a horrible thing to happen, and I understand your reluctance to deal with Lidell before you're certain the pregnancy will come to term. But I also think you prefer to ignore what makes you uncomfortable in favor of concentrating on things that bring you joy. Sometimes to the detriment of everyone around you and to your own goals. You did that with Nathan. You're doing it with Adrien and with Lidell."

"I want to be happy, too, Simon. Am I not allowed a little of that? After all I've been through with Nathan and losing him, after dealing with Lidell and Ned's misery-inducing complaints and problems for years, and after giving up my dreams of being an architect to run a musty old family estate, don't I deserve to wallow in some pleasure and joy?"

Simon's jowls jiggled again as he seemed to work out a suitable reply. "I always wish for your joy, but you bring much of that pain on yourself by refusing to face and deal with it from the start. If you'd accepted Nathan for who he was, hadn't tried to change him, or if—"

"Don't!" Heath said, putting out his hand to stop the unwanted flow of words. "I'm late."

"By refusing to hear me out, you're doing exactly what I'm saying you shouldn't: ignoring pain in hopes that it will simply go away if you don't attend to it."

Heath turned on his heel, left Simon sighing in the entryway, and stomped out into the sun again. The car was waiting for him, and he pulled away from Clearwater Castle with his pulse thrumming.

Heath just wanted peace. Was that too much to ask? He wanted to spend the next few months of Adrien's pregnancy enjoying the simple things, learning the man's body and mind, hearing stories of his past, and maybe, just maybe starting to spin some hopes for their future.

Reality had a place in the future. He would eventually have to inform his brother and Ned about the changes in their fortunes, but there was no need to rush it. As for talking to Adrien about Nathan, obviously there would come a day when he would need to explain. After all, if they did build something together, if their paths intertwined as a couple in the future, there would be no way to prevent Adrien from meeting Heath's friends and family, all of whom would see the resemblance immediately.

But there was no need to rush that. They had months still, and Adrien was in the early stages of his pregnancy. There was no need to upset him just yet.

For a fleeting moment, Heath wondered how much it would cost him to bribe all of his friends and family to simply forget that Nathan had ever existed and to embrace Adrien without revealing the truth. But even he knew that was impossible.

The question of when to tell Adrien was an important one; the timing would need to be just right. He'd never intended for his heart to get involved or to even entertain the idea of Adrien being in his life going forward. He still wasn't sure it would even play out that way. Adrien was easy to be with, and he'd taken to being cared for like a duck to water, but pregnancy hormones make all omegas pliant, amiable. Don't they?

Heath scrubbed a hand over his face, wishing that he had simply told Adrien up front. Then there would be no question at all. Why hadn't he foreseen that living with a pregnant, beautiful, willing, open-hearted, innocent omega might wake his heart from its slumber? It seemed obvious in retrospect.

All he knew for sure was that now was not the time to stir the pot.

Drawing up to the glittering high-rise where his first appointment of the day awaited, Heath straightened his tie and tried to pull his thoughts together. Damn Simon for getting him riled up after such a blissful morning spent cuddling naked with Adrien, laughing and licking fresh fruit juice out of his ripe, red mouth.

As he stepped out of the car, he nodded firmly. Simon was right in one way: everyone would have to know the truth eventually. But he was wrong in another: no one needed to know right now.

Heath made his choice.

Confession could wait.

# Chapter Fifteen

ADRIEN RAN HIS hand along the wall of concrete tunnel between the door that led to the larger part of the castle, back down to his bedroom, and out to the living room. Simon was in the garden pruning the roses, and he was inside wearing the soft, light robe that Heath had bought for him. Underneath, he was naked as a jaybird. The robe fluttered around his calves as he made what was becoming his daily meditative walk.

He turned around and headed back up the tunnel, his fingers trailing in and out of different colors of light funneled in from the high windows and the skylights above. Amber light, golden light, a creamy white that made his pale fingers look white as milk. He counted the steps as he walked, making a little song in his head.

The tunnel was comforting. It smelled of trapped cooking scents, usually whatever Simon had made that morning. Today, it smelled of freshly baked bread, yeasty and delicious, warm and homey. The day before it had smelled of peaches. He wasn't sure what he found so perfect about light in the tunnel, but it was mesmerizing to him. He could walk the tunnel over and over, but the light was never the same twice, shifting as the sun moved outside and the angles changed too.

His two favorite places were the garden, with all the roses of different colors and scents, and the tunnel. In both places, he could relax his mind, breathe in and out, and simply let all the worries, questions, nagging concerns slip away like so much flotsam.

"You look beautiful in that light, little one."

Heath's voice brought Adrien out of his reverent study of the light, and he smiled to see his alpha standing at the end of the hallway. "You look handsome in that suit." He waggled his brows as Heath strode to join him. "I want to rub all over it."

Heath grabbed him in a kiss, and Adrien did just that, brushing his sensitive skin against the material that smelled so strongly of his alpha. It was a good, soft wool suit, made with quality and care. In his infatuation with Heath's suits, Adrien thought that when he returned to school, he might change his study focus from the cultural meaning in the design choices of Hontu handwoven fabrics and material art to studying the cultural meaning attached to the design of men's suits. But that was bordering on a fashion focus and not an artistic one, not to mention it felt a bit fetishistic, given his current reaction to Heath in a suit.

"A quick fuck before dinner?" Adrien begged.

"No," Heath said, a quiver of amusement in his voice. "First, a walk in the garden, conversation, and then we'll bond our flesh."

"But I want you." Adrien flicked what he hoped was a sexy look from beneath his lashes.

Heath growled. "I want you too, but you'll follow my commands. Understand?"

Adrien's knees went weak. He loved following Heath's commands. Though he couldn't say just why, exactly. It made him feel safe, like he had when he was a child and his father told him what to do, how to think, and what to feel. Eventually, that had chafed when he hit adolescence, and he'd found his father's commanding attitude stifling. But now, pregnant and ripening, a little frightened but willing to trust Heath, he found his commands intoxicating.

So he gave in to them without too much thought.

Seeing that Heath was with Adrien, Simon left them alone. The garden was beautiful, and the roses ruffled in the breeze all around. Adrien removed his robe and left it on a bench, enjoying the gust of air on his skin. He could almost feel the sweet perfume of the roses, it floated so thickly around him, and reached out his hand to fondle a big bloom.

"What did you do today?" he asked Heath as he bent to take a deeper sniff of the red rose.

"Attended appointments in the city, visited my nephew's school to clear up a problem there, and argued with Simon." Heath said the last reluctantly, and he plucked the rose, using his nails to dislodge the thorns, before putting it behind Adrien's ear.

"Arguing with Simon about what?"

"About the future. I haven't told my brother yet about the baby."

"Won't he be happy for you?"

"He'll be furious," Heath said, his mouth widening in a tight smile. "Utterly enraged."

"Why?" Adrien was mystified. He'd always believed that babies were a gift. That's what his father had taught him and what the religion of his youth had touted. He'd never thought of a child as anything but something to celebrate, even if he, himself, had often been terrified by the prospect of growing one inside his body and birthing it.

"Because his son Ned is my current heir. Once this little one is born"—Heath touched Adrien's stomach, his warm fingers stroking over the hair between Adrien's navel and his pubic mound—"Lidell's son will be displaced. You can see how that might get under his skin."

Adrien frowned. "He must have expected you to try for a

child yourself one day?" It seemed obvious to him that Heath would want an heir of his own. It was what every alpha was supposed to strive for, and it was taken for granted that every alpha would do just that.

"I may have made dramatic, emotional statements in the past when I was grieving that led him to believe otherwise."

"Ah." Adrien didn't like to think of the baby Heath and his other omega had lost. It felt like it might jinx things for him, bring bad energy to his own pregnancy, and so he refused to ponder it much. But of course Heath had grieved the loss. He was selfish not to have considered how much it must have hurt him.

Heath touched Adrien's cheek. "Do you think I should tell my brother?"

"I think that we have a lot of time yet before we'll know if the baby will be born healthy, or if it will be an alpha so it can inherit—"

"I don't believe in those laws."

Adrien's heart fluttered. "You believe omegas should be allowed to inherit?"

"I believe that my own child should take precedence of another no matter the sex."

Adrien nodded, thinking about Heath's words about Lidell. "Your brother's anger would make you unhappy, and if you were unhappy that would bring tension into the nest. Maybe I'm selfish to say this, but I don't know that causing your brother upset would really be beneficial to anyone right now. Once the child is born, healthy and strong, then you will have a better position to endure his rage. Don't you think?"

"So you advocate keeping our nest free of upset?"

"Until the baby comes," Adrien said, touching his stomach, which had started to feel taut from the pressure inside but which wasn't bulging quite yet. "I have put aside my worries about school and my fears for the future. I've taken your command to enjoy myself to heart. I want you, as much as possible, to do the same."

Heath studied Adrien's face intently and then nodded. "I'll do all I can to keep your nest a place of peace."

Adrien smiled and leaned against Heath. He nuzzled his neck, enjoying the soft scrape of his suit against skin. "Our nest," he corrected. "I'm still pretending this is the place you built for me, for us."

Heath wrapped his arms around Adrien and pulled him close. "You don't need to pretend. This nest has never seen a happier moment than the ones we share together." They stood in the soft evening sun, the rosebushes casting shadows that danced on Adrien's skin.

"Did I tell you I used to want to be an architect?" Heath asked. "That I designed this nest myself?"

"No," Adrien said, looking up with wonder. "Tell me about it now."

They found a bench in the gazebo. Heath stroked Adrien's naked body as he talked, bringing him up to a full erection. Adrien asked halting questions as Heath chatted like he wasn't also erect inside his suit. "And then my parents died, and my duties as heir took over my life."

"You were passionate about it," Adrien said, squirming as Heath began giving him a slow hand job.

"I still enjoy dabbling in design. I'd like to build a house away from here one day. I've never loved living in this rococo monstrosity."

"What kind of house?"

"I'm not sure yet. When I decide, I'll start drafting plans for it." He rubbed his thumb over Adrien's cock, smearing the precum around the head.

"When I was younger, I used to dream at night about a

house," Adrien said, his hips shifting up and down in rhythm. "Not fantasize, dream. When I was asleep."

"What was it like?"

"By the sea. Open. Broad. A lot of light." Adrien moaned and turned his face to hide it in Heath's neck. "I'm going to come."

"Yes, I think you should."

"I want to come with your cock in me."

"That can happen later. Tell me more about this house."

"The light was changeable…like…like the tunnel. Oh!" Adrien gripped Heath's suit jacket, crying out against Heath's neck, and orgasmed hard. Cum shot up in the space between them, and then fell, marking Heath's beautiful suit pants.

"That's good," Heath whispered as Adrien came down from the sweet high. He indicated the cum on his pants. "Lick that up."

Adrien hunched over and complied. His cum tasted different now that he was pregnant. It was less harsh like a salt-and-sour kick, more alluring like the sea. He hummed softly, wishing it was Heath's cum, though. That always settled him down. Kept him flying high.

"You're a good boy," Heath whispered. "I could grow to…"

Adrien looked up, his heart feeling like it had been hooked by a fishing rod and jerked onto dry land. *Please*, he wanted to say. *Please say you could care for me.*

"You must be hungry to eat that up so fast." Heath tugged Adrien to his feet. "Let's go inside. Over dinner, I want to hear about your studies at school. You mentioned Hontu fabric the other day. What drew you to that?"

Adrien let himself be led inside, his balls buzzing with recent release and his body singing joyfully. He didn't know what the future would bring, but this time-out from life was beautiful, and being with Heath only made it better.

He didn't want anything to disturb it.

# Chapter Sixteen

IT WAS HARD to believe that just under four months ago, Adrien hadn't even been in Ron Finch's office yet. His life had been so normal then. He'd woken up every morning, showered, eaten breakfast in the dorm, and gone to his classes. He'd been consumed by the questions of Hontu design, fascinated by the details of his studies. He'd hung on the lectures of his professors like his father had hung on the words of the preacher. Like they spoke the word of God.

Now, rubbing his gradually expanding stomach, he had a hard time understanding what had seemed so important in all that academia, what had held his attention so tenaciously. This new life, his changing body, and his slow-growing relationship with Heath seemed much more compelling. The inner world of his heart and mind, the development of the child inside, the small movements he was beginning to feel, and the peaceful pace of his thoughts were addictive.

His current life was far from dynamic. It was, if anything, even more steady and easygoing than the way he'd lived before. There was no pressure to be anywhere or do anything other than what pleased him. The academic world seemed fuzzy and almost silly in the scheme of the beautiful, endless mystery of generating new life.

None of the science he'd studied could fully explain the animalistic urges inside him to bond with Heath, to fuck and suck, or explain his sense of the growing child's nature, already so different from his own. Life was slow and sensual now, but there was something new every day—in his body, in his small world of the nest Heath had built for this purpose.

The blossoms of the roses, the caterpillars, the butterflies, and the bluebird feather found on the bench in the gazebo kept him company while he sat naked most afternoons feeling the cooling breeze against his hot skin. His baby was moving inside of him now, shifting languidly from one side to another, and he loved the flutter and kicks. They made him feel simultaneously tiny and infinite, tied to the universe yet just a speck of it. He sometimes got a glimpse of the world from so far away that it was as though he were in the stars, and what he saw was the same across species: life striving for life. It was simple and stunning.

He was calm more often than not despite having not left the nest to even explore the castle. Heath had been right: the semen he swallowed or had deposited up his ass kept him sated and happy. It was almost like a drug, he supposed. But he couldn't be bothered to really mind it.

Everything about his life now was sweet, and he couldn't help but want it to last.

"Adrien," Simon said, stepping out of the nest with his butler's outfit askew. Heath had suggested he stop wearing it while taking care of Adrien, since they kept the nest so hot for Adrien's comfort, but the old man was set in his ways and refused to completely let it go. He did unbutton and untuck his shirt, sometimes, to waft in some cooler air against his skin, and he carried a fan, too.

"Yes, Simon?"

"Dinner is ready. Unfortunately, lovey, Heath won't be here tonight with you. He sends his greatest sorrow and wants you to know he'll be back before the night is up, but he's been called to the city to deal with a problem regarding his nephew." Simon frowned. "He's a disaster in the making, that one is. But that's what we all said about Heath, too, and he's turned out just fine."

Adrien's ears perked up at the mention of Heath's younger days. He'd wanted to know so much more about his alpha's life before him, but Heath was tight-lipped about much of it, saying it didn't matter anymore. The future, the baby, and what they shared right now was the most important thing, he claimed. He often reminded Adrien, too, of his own words about wanting to keep the nest peaceful for the pregnancy, claiming the past was an unnecessary hornet's nest and it was best not to kick it.

For the most part, Adrien understood. He didn't want to spend a lot of time talking about his lost father, the years of loneliness on the farm, or retraining his brain from the religious doctrine he'd been spoon-fed since infancy, either. But there was so much more to Heath's life, being older. Adrien had more years ahead of him than behind, and hopefully Heath did, too, but surely there was some interesting history there?

Simon had turned to go back inside, but Adrien stopped him. "Stay, Simon. Sit in here with me. There's a nice breeze through the forest today, and the shade beneath the gazebo roof is almost chilly."

"Are you cold? I'll fetch you the silk robe—"

"No," Adrien called out, patting the bench.

He did enjoy the silk robe Heath had brought for him, though he'd long ago stopped feeling shy about his nudity in front of Simon. Not after Simon had walked in on all manner of activities with Heath during the last few months, and not after his skin on his stomach had started really stretching with the baby and the rest of him came alight like exposed nerve endings. Still, he did sometimes slide the soft robe on when he was chilled, but today he enjoyed the breeze across his skin, raising his nipples and ruffling his hair. It made him feel alive.

"Just sit with me."

Simon crossed over to him, bypassing some of Adrien's favorite roses, red blowsy ones with a scent that made him moan, and took up a place in the shade across from Adrien. He fanned himself with his small fan and leaned back with his ankles crossed.

"Do you want to stay for dinner with me?" Adrien asked. He didn't like to think of himself as needy. In the past he'd always been content alone, but now he was accustomed to spending his days reading or contemplating the clouds in the sky while feeling his baby move and the evenings lost in Heath's company. An evening alone, too, seemed like too much.

"That is a kind offer," Simon said, rubbing his jowl and smiling kindly. "You're a sweet man. I'm afraid I have other obligations in the evenings, however."

He'd never wondered much before about Simon's afterhours, where he went, or what he did, but suddenly he was curious about them. Did he eat alone at night or with the other servants of the big castle, always invisible since the first day? Or did he even live in the big place? Maybe he had a house on the estate somewhere or in the city. Perhaps a lover or a spouse. No children, though. As a beta, he couldn't have any.

"Do you have someone waiting for you?"

"You could say that," Simon said elusively. "Heath won't be very late. You could watch a movie, maybe. I noticed that you've barely touched the entertainment console in your room."

Adrien shrugged. He liked to live in his dreamy, quiet contentedness during the day, and at night Heath took far too much attention, what with his hard cock and strong arms and rapid-fire fucking. He felt his face flush at the memory and crossed his legs to hide his cock's reaction. "I might. Or I could read some more."

He returned to his original reason to call Simon over. "Or…I was wondering…does Heath have any old photo albums? From his youth or teen years, that is? Not recent digital pictures. Older than that." He smiled. "I've been curious lately what the baby might look like." It seemed a good enough excuse to want to see and didn't sound as pathetic as admitting that Heath barely told him anything about his history.

"He does, yes," Simon said. "Would you like me to get them for you?"

"Do you think Heath would mind?" That was a risky question, he knew, the one that might get this opportunity to explore even a little of Heath's past revoked, but he wouldn't have felt right not asking it.

"He might," Simon said with a thoughtful expression. "But he hasn't forbidden it. In fact, I've been instructed to give you anything you ask for."

"Oh." He sat in silence, Simon's eyes on him intensely. Finally, he said, "Will he be angry if I look at them?"

"Have you ever seen Heath angry?"

Adrien thought back to when he'd first met Heath, being ordered to show his hole, kneeling in the dirt to suck his cock, and then being fucked in the entry of the heat cabin as he felt the first real swells of the heat. He'd been hard, rough, perfunctory, but never angry. Never cruel or outright mean.

"No," he said softly.

"It's a rare event, but it does happen. I can't tell you how he'd feel about you looking at the photos or what his reaction will be, but I can say that if you ask for them, I'll bring them to you before I leave for the night." Simon fanned himself more vigorously. Adrien tried to determine if it was due to nerves or heat.

"I'd like to look at the photos, please." What harm could it do? He couldn't imagine there would be anything in a family photo album that would be embarrassing or shameful. And if there was, then Adrien would just have to find the box of his things from his dorm where he'd shoved the photo albums he'd salvaged from his father's house after his death. There were a good number of silly photos of him as a kid in there. Tit for tat.

"I'll have the albums to you by nightfall. I'll send Jonas with them."

"Jonas?" Adrien said, uncrossing his legs and enjoying the wind fluttering through his hair.

"He's a young servant here. An alpha, actually. Heath is going to train him up to work in the business, but for now he keeps the files in Heath's office."

"Oh, Heath has an office..." Adrien trailed off. "I assumed his office was in the city."

"He works from home most of the time."

All day long while Adrien lolled about in the nest and the garden, Heath was on the same property? Somehow, he felt snubbed that he didn't know this information before now. "Oh. What does he do in his office here?"

"He takes appointments, there's always someone wanting to meet with him, and phone calls. Everyone wants to talk with him about investing in their schemes."

"Does he? Invest in people's 'schemes'?"

"Sometimes. And sometimes not." Simon heaved himself up. "Now, I'll tell Jonas to put the books in your bedroom. If you stay out here for another half hour or so, Adrien, you won't have to worry about putting on the robe. He'll be down and gone again."

Adrien cradled his stomach, holding his hand over a spot where the baby was kicking in little flutters. He saw Simon hesitate, watching curiously. "He's kicking," he explained.

Simon tilted his head. "Does it hurt?"

"No." Adrien looked up at Simon and saw the bare curiosity on his face. "Have you ever felt a baby move?"

Simon shook his head.

"Come here," Adrien said, reaching out for Simon's hand. It was soft but starting to get arthritis in some of the joints. He placed the old man's hand on his stomach and hoped the baby wouldn't get shy now.

"Oh!" Simon said, jerking his hand back when the baby gave a good kick. "That's strong!"

"Yeah," Adrien said, grinning helplessly. He stroked his stomach again. "He's busy today."

"Enjoying the fresh air, as he should," Simon said, straightening up and lifting his wobbly chin. "Good evening, lovey. I'll see you in the morning."

Adrien lingered in the garden until the sun started to set, and he did grow chilly. He went inside and ate the dinner Simon had prepared for him: cold salad and a delicious cheese-and-meat plate. He made himself walk around the living area, pretending that he might read a book or sit down on the sofa, but eventually he eagerly raced back to his bedroom.

The window screens were drawn, probably Simon's doing. He knew that it unnerved Adrien to walk into the room at night and made him feel exposed to the forest. On the center of his bed were four thick photo albums, and he heaved them up into his arms, resting them on his stomach as he walked back into the cozy living room to take his time looking at them.

Each album was navy-blue leather with a white label card on the front. The first card displayed dates that, if Adrien had guessed Heath's age correctly, probably started right before or after his birth and went through the years of his childhood. The next two labels displayed dates in a different hand and seemed to correspond with high school, college, and young manhood. The fourth label, though, held a name and no dates. It simply said *Nathan*.

Adrien started on the first album. Some of the photos there were black-and-white but clearly post-War. Everyone wore the waist-high trousers that were common and the striped button-up shirts that had been all the rage then. His own father had had some similar-looking pictures from his youth.

Baby Heath was a chubby little thing. His omega parent held him in most of the pictures; there was one of him still chestfeeding at what appeared to be almost three years old. That was a devoted omega. That was love.

Adrien felt an odd pang for the man who'd given birth to him and then left before the year was up. What would it have been like to be cherished like Heath so clearly had been? Would he be a different sort of man now? He rubbed his own stomach and felt a vow growing in his heart, but he kept it back, a lingering fear keeping him from voicing it aloud even to himself.

Not yet.

Little boy Heath was wild, it seemed. Shaggy dark hair and eyes that gleamed with mischief. There was a string of photos of him racing around the grounds, just a blur of a boy holding a sharp stick and wearing sturdy boots. And there was a young Simon! Rushing after him, looking dapper in his nurse uniform, while Heath's omega parent looked on laughing.

Adrien smiled fondly. How devoted Simon must be. Heath must be like his son.

He cracked open the next book, amused to find that puberty didn't treat Heath well at all. His nose was too big, his face marred by pimples, and yet he stared unflinchingly, confidently into the camera, and even over the distance of years that expression made Adrien melt inside. "Yes, sir," he whispered, saluting the man who'd so easily mastered him. He had no doubt he could have done the very same in his youth.

The photos from the college years were a bit horrifying. Adrien had heard rumors that parties like these took place at his school, but he'd kept his head down and ignored it all. Heath, apparently, hadn't.

"Wow." Adrien hummed, flipping past the pages of Heath-behaving-badly until he reached some pages near the middle of the third book of Heath traveling the world.

He ran his fingers over the photos of Heath in a bathing suit on white sand with a blue sea in the background. Heath with a backpack at a mountain peak, grinning like a hopeless fool at whoever was taking the photo and spreading his arms wide, as if he was saying, "I'm giving you this whole wide world."

Adrien felt a tug of jealousy for whoever Heath had looked at like that.

Then he started to notice that every second or third picture was missing from the album. Just a blank spot where a picture should have been. He frowned, wondering what—or who—had been removed.

His mind skittered to the fourth album.

Was it Nathan?

He reached for the blue leather album with the man's name on top and pulled it into his lap.

"What are you doing?"

Adrien jumped, his hand flying to his chest, and the baby thumping hard as the push of adrenaline woke him up.

"I didn't mean to scare you," Heath said, loosening his tie and walking toward Adrien with a sweet smile on his face. "Are you feeling okay?"

"Yes, yeah," Adrien said, putting the photo albums aside for now. "Just looking at pictures of you as a baby." He motioned toward the blue leather volumes.

Heath stopped mid-step and glanced down at them, too, and then continued walking. "Oh, yeah? Where'd you get those?"

Something in his voice was cautious.

"Simon had Jonas bring them down."

"Jonas?" Heath asked, nostrils flaring, as he raked his gaze over Adrien's naked body. "He's an alpha. No other alpha should see—"

"I was in the gazebo. My nakedness is still for your eyes only," Adrien said, chuckling. "And Simon's."

"Simon doesn't count."

Adrien sat back on the sofa, pulling the first book over again. "You should be ashamed of saying that about the man who cleaned all this mud off you," he said, opening it to a page with a photo of a half-naked Heath being scrubbed off in a garden fountain by a very annoyed-looking Simon, while, yet again, his omega parent looked on laughing. Another stab of envy went through Adrien. He wondered what his own omega parent looked like when he laughed. Another thing he'd never know. Another mystery he'd have to surrender to.

"Poor Simon," Heath agreed, taking the book from Adrien's hand and shoving the rest aside. Heath took Adrien's glasses off and set them aside. Then turned back to gaze down at him as he continued to work to get off his clothes. He smirked at Adrien. "If only you knew all the hell I've given him over the years."

"I can guess." Adrien's nipples and cock tingled under Heath's watch, and both raised up hard and tight.

"Mmm." Heath was naked now, showing off his hairy chest and muscled stomach, his taut thighs, looking especially delicious tonight. Adrien ran his hands up and down his flanks, enjoying the way Heath's cock rose in front of his face, just begging to be licked. "Suck me," Heath said, taking hold of Adrien's hair.

"Make me wet for you."

Adrien's ass leaked slick, and his nipples grew even more taut. He opened his mouth for Heath and moaned as his thickness invaded deep. He whimpered as pre-cum striped his tongue, and he worked Heath into the back of his throat, sticking out his tongue to paint his balls.

"I want to fuck you," Heath grunted, slowly fucking his throat instead. "Make you come on my dick. Watch you writhe." He gripped Adrien's hair hard. "Moan for me, slut."

Adrien obeyed, and Heath hissed out, "Fuck," as his balls drew up. He pulled free of Adrien's mouth, bent low to kiss him, and then tugged Adrien up to standing. He ran his hands all over Adrien's body, lavishing attention on his stomach, feeling the baby's movements under the skin.

"You woke him up," Adrien rasped, his cock aching. "He was asleep until you scared me."

"Then we'll rock him back to sleep," Heath said, his voice sending a shiver down Adrien's back and making his asshole twitch and leak. "Get on my dick."

Adrien hurried to turn around, putting his hands on the back of the sofa and his knees on the seat. He liked it this way best now that his stomach had grown so big. The angle of Heath's cock stroked against his prostate just right and he was able to come without jerking off if Heath went at it hard and relentlessly. And the way Heath was talking to him, Adrien didn't think he'd have to worry about that tonight.

"Stick it out," Heath muttered, stroking a hand down Adrien's back to grip his ass and shake it a little. "Look at that sweet hole. Such a hot cocksleeve."

Adrien shuddered again. The dirty things Heath called him always lit him up inside and had since the time in the heat cabin. He had a secret hope, a fruitless wish, that Heath had saved those filthy terms just for him, that he was the first to hear them. He knew it wasn't true, and yet he wanted it so badly.

"Have you been a good boy today?" Heath asked, sliding his fingers in and out of Adrien's slick hole. "Do you deserve your alpha's cock?"

"Yes," Adrien whimpered, pushing back. "I need it."

"Mm, but do you *deserve* it?"

"Yes!"

"Who pried into my past without asking?"

Adrien stiffened slightly. The baby went still, too. "I did."

"Did you find what you were looking for?" Heath asked. He sounded colder than he had since they'd first met.

"Yes," Adrien said uncertainly.

"And what was that?"

"Pictures of you growing up. In high school. College."

"What else?"

"Traveling." Adrien licked his lips, wanting to ask about the missing pictures, but instead he said, "I want to go to the beach one day. I've never been."

Heath finger fucked Adrien lazily, his silence stretching out, until Adrien put his head down on his hands, gripping the back of the sofa, and relaxed into the electric bliss of his prostate being rubbed.

"I'll take you to the beach," Heath finally said. "And the mountains. I'll take you anywhere you want to go." He slapped Adrien's ass. "Now climb on."

Adrien whimpered and pushed back, searching for the blunt tip of Heath's cock and groaning when he finally encountered it. Heath shoved it directly in, long, fat, and so damn hard.

"Yes," Adrien said, rolling his hips on Heath's dick, doing the work to get that cockhead to fly over his prostate.

"Fuck," Heath said from behind him. "Hungry hole tonight."

"So hungry," Adrien grunted, as he worked his ass up and down, rolled it and rocked it, and tried to drive Heath out of his mind as he sought his own orgasm.

The weight of his growing stomach rocked back and forth, and Heath gripped Adrien's hips, bent low over him, and kissed his shoulder blades. Adrien smiled into his hands, his body thrilled to be fucked, his heart pleased with the affection. When Heath pulled him up to standing, his ass aching on Heath's big cock, he wrenched around and stood on his toes to take his kiss.

Tongues and lips moved together, his ass throbbing around Heath's penetration, and Adrien was in heaven. "I love you," he whispered, working his ass again and turning back to grip the couch.

Heath's hips stuttered, but then he fucked Adrien even more vigorously. He reached around and tweaked Adrien's nipples, working them fiercely, until they burned and ached, making him keen. Heath hissed suddenly, and Adrien felt something hot and wet leak from his nipples. He gasped, stopped twisting his hips on Heath's cock, and looked down to where Heath was still pinching and working him.

Milk seeped from his nipples, hot and sweet-scented.

"My beautiful omega," Heath said, tweaking his nipples even more roughly so that additional milk leaked out. "Your body is a miracle."

Adrien moaned, his nipples aching and tingling, his cock thudding with desire.

"Come on my cock," Heath commanded. "Show me how you make yourself come."

As Heath twisted his nipples and milk dripped onto the sofa, Adrien worked himself on Heath's cock, the stinging bliss of his hole taking him high and releasing him again and again. His balls felt so full, and then the tight throb began deep and he tossed his head back, rolling his hips. He froze as Heath grabbed him by the shoulders and fucked into him hard, hard, hard.

Adrien yelled, his body convulsing, his womb tightening, and his asshole spasming. He came like the end of the world, his vision whiting out, as cum spurted from his cock and his nipples tingled and gushed along with his ass. He was a mess of fluids, and yet he felt so good as he wrung himself out on Heath's still-plunging dick.

"Yes," Heath gritted out, burrowing in deep. "That's right. My omega. My Adrien," he said, and then he collapsed on Adrien's back, grunting as he filled him up with powerful spurts of cum.

Adrien missed being knotted, but being held in Heath's arms while still impaled on his dick was almost as good. He couldn't wait until his next heat, whenever that would be, so he could feel Heath's knot again.

He drifted on the fantasy for a long time, slipping sideways on the wide sofa and wrapping his arms around his belly. The baby was quiet now, rocked to sleep like Heath had said, either by their thrusts or the spasms of his womb.

Heath kissed the top of Adrien's head. "If you want to know about my past, ask. Don't get Simon to bring you things."

"I'm sorry," Adrien said softly.

Heath sighed. "It's all right. It's just that we have such a short time left. I don't want it spoiled with things that don't matter."

Adrien turned those words over in his mind. He was due in less time now than he'd been here. He was past the halfway mark. And then what happened? What would become of him, them, the baby? Heath had said he'd take him anywhere in the world, but that had been in the heat of the moment. Adrien knew he couldn't trust that.

He thought of dreams he'd been indulging in only moments

earlier, of being knotted during heat by Heath again. What if that's not what Heath wanted? He said they had a short time together now.

Adrien squeezed his ass around Heath's softening cock. He'd have to enjoy every last bit of it while he could. Because who knew what was ahead?

# Chapter Seventeen

HEATH FELT ASSURED that Adrien at least had some clue as to what to expect now that they'd read through the entire pregnancy and delivery portions of the book. Still, the boy had obviously been surprised when his nipples had overflowed as they fucked. He wanted to reassure him, but Adrien was quiet and sleepy now. Just one of the delightful aftereffects of fucking him.

He carefully rolled off Adrien and carried him to his bedroom. "I'll be right back, little one," he said. "I haven't eaten. Rest here, and we'll read a bit more."

He wasn't hungry at all, but he didn't want the photo albums lingering. He still wasn't sure how to explain to Adrien about Nathan; he only knew that he should have by now, and that by waiting so long he had made it all that much more awkward and potentially upsetting. Which was what Simon had told him from the beginning.

Fucking Simon.

Simon had known that if Adrien looked at all those albums, if he opened the one with Nathan's name, he'd see what everyone else who'd known Nathan had seen immediately—the resemblance between the two of them. And he'd know that Heath and Nathan had been lovers. There were photos that…well, there were photos of some very pleasurable moments they'd thought to catch on film. And now he thought it might be best to burn the entire album just to be safe.

He caught it up in one hand, determined to take it upstairs, summon a staff member, and order them to do just that, when the album fell open and he was struck dumb staring down at the page.

Nathan laughing.

He was beautiful. It made Heath's stomach tense up with an echo of grief. He touched Nathan's smile, the crinkle in his eyes, and ached with the loss of it again. Adrien should have known him. He would have liked his omega parent.

Heath huffed. And where would that have left him? Adrien wouldn't be his now, wouldn't be growing so beautifully round with his child if Nathan had kept a relationship with his son. That would have been taboo.

Perhaps it was still taboo.

He snapped the book shut, determined to hide it at least.

"Did you love him very much?" Adrien asked. He stood by the corner of the hall that led to his room wearing the silk robe and his glasses. The robe looked so lovely against his skin. "The man in that book? Nathan?"

Heath blinked at him. "Did you look at this one?" he asked gruffly.

"No. I was about to, but…" Adrien stepped forward, reaching out to the book. Heath kept it from his hands. "You took all the pictures of him out of the other album and put them in here. Why?"

"He's dead."

"Oh." Adrien pulled his hand back. "I'm sorry."

"Yes, well…" He shrugged.

"So you took the pictures out so you only had to see him if you wanted to. To contain the way you feel the hurt?" Adrien asked. "I get that. I did something similar with my dad's stuff. I put it all in a box and—" He broke off.

Heath stared at him, the intelligent innocence of his eyes behind his glasses, and he thought he should just tell him the truth. Get it all out in the open. But he didn't want to ruin these last few weeks together. The baby would come and then…then he could be honest and see how Adrien reacted. There was no use in telling him now. It changed nothing—not what he'd felt, what they'd done, or what they'd made together.

"I loved him," Heath said. "He's dead. End of story."

He almost wanted to punch himself because it was far from the end of the story, and he knew it, but he didn't want to talk about Nathan tonight. The truth was too close to the surface, and he loved Adrien too much to give up what little time they had left.

Wait. Loved him? He *loved* him?

Adrien had said it while they fucked, but….

"I'm sorry I invaded your privacy." Adrien pushed his glasses up the bridge of his nose. It was a movement that made Heath's heart wrench with affection.

"I love you," Heath said sharply. "You should know that." He nodded firmly. "So there. I love you."

Adrien's eyes went wide, and his plump mouth fell open. Heath wished he had it in him to fuck that mouth again tonight, but he would be lucky to plug Adrien's hole again in the middle of the night, the way he often craved. It had been a very long day.

"Oh, well, I love you, too," Adrien said, but his eyes were wet. He smiled wide and shiny at Heath, the photo album and dead man clearly forgotten. "I love you too."

Heath took his omega back to bed and read to him from the pregnancy book until he fell asleep. This time about what to expect post-partum, how to feed the baby, and what they could expect from the child the first few months.

The next section, though, was the scary part. It talked about the plans the alpha and omega parent should make for the future. Heath considered himself a brave, strong man with a stupidly passionate heart, but if Adrien didn't want to stay and raise their baby, if he didn't want to make more children with Heath and marry him, then he simply didn't know what he'd do with himself.

He kissed Adrien's soft hair and shut the book. But that was something else that could wait for another night.

"HE DIDN'T LIKE that I looked at the photo albums," Adrien said as Simon scrambled eggs. He sipped from his juice and watched the milk-and-egg combination go into the skillet, and then he sat down at the counter to wait.

"Did you see anything interesting in them?" Simon asked, with a certain stiffness in his voice that Adrien took for anxiety.

"I liked the pictures of him as a young boy. And you were very handsome back then. Not that you're not handsome now!"

Simon chortled. "Oh, I well remember how old men look to the young. I *was* handsome, though, wasn't I? My Earl certainly thought so."

"Oh, so you do have a lover?"

"A lover?" Simon laughed again. "Earl and I have been married for forty years. Lover…pfft." He worked the eggs expertly in the skillet and then slid them onto a plate for Adrien to eat.

"What does Earl think of Heath?"

"He thinks he's spoiled," Simon said obviously without a care about how that might sound. "And he *is* spoiled, but he's a good man. Devoted. Loyal." He said that intently, with a particular gaze at Adrien.

"Yes, I can see that." He rested his hand on his stomach as he ate. The baby flipped around inside, shoving off his liver. He tapped himself and sighed contentedly. He even liked when the little booger hurt him.

"Sometimes Heath makes poor choices, rash ones, but he's a good man."

"Of course."

"I'm glad you know that."

Adrien pondered his eggs and then decided to just ask. "Who was Nathan? His lover, I know, but how long were they together? How did they meet?"

Simon froze and stared at him. "So you saw the pictures of Nathan, then?"

"No. He'd removed them from the books I got a chance to see. He came in and found me looking just as I was getting ready to open the one with Nathan's name on it. Now, it's gone." Not that he'd planned to look this morning. It was clear that it upset Heath for him to pry. And yet…

Here he was prying again.

"So they were in love, then?"

"Heath was in love. Nathan was greedy." Simon frowned. "Don't get me wrong. Nathan was a delight to be around socially. Made me laugh like there was no tomorrow. But, in the end, he liked Heath's money and his cock, and that was about all he truly cared about."

Adrien gaped. He'd never heard Simon be so crude before.

"Truth isn't pretty," Simon said as if he was dusting his hands of the whole thing. "What did Heath say when you asked him about Nathan?"

Adrien poked at his eggs, feeling restless and not as hungry as usual. "He said he was dead. That he'd loved him, but he was dead."

Simon snorted. "Just like Heath to be so brutally succinct."

"He said he loved me," Adrien whispered, his eyes down. A smile broke over his lips, and he poked at his eggs again. He took off his glasses and set them aside, wiping at his suddenly damp eyes. "He said it twice."

Simon laughed and squeezed Adrien's hand. "I could have told you that."

"Really?"

"It's been evident."

"How?"

"Are you so oblivious?" Simon rolled his eyes, which, even blurry, looked sort of silly on a man of his age.

"So you think he'll want me to stay? He won't send me away or expect me to leave him behind?" Adrien stroked his stomach again. "The baby, I mean, or Heath, for that matter."

"I doubt very much that he'll want you to ever leave. I suspect that choice will be up to you."

"I want to stay with him."

"What about your studies and school? You auctioned your heat and breeding to become a professor. What of that?"

"What does that matter?" Adrien asked, dreamily, his fingers tracing his stomach softly, his heart a pulpy mess of affection for the life inside and for Heath. "Our family matters more."

"Oh, boy. Those pregnancy hormones sure do a number on men. Alphas and omegas alike. I'm telling you now, keep your options open. Don't make promises you won't want to keep."

"The rest of the world just doesn't seem to matter," Adrien said again. He pushed his glasses even farther away on the counter and turned his attention back to his stomach. "Not when I feel happy here. Safe and content. What's wrong with wanting that? For me and for my baby?"

"Nothing is wrong with it. But life isn't about safety. And feelings change."

"Not my feelings," Adrien said, and even as the words came out of his mouth he felt both certain and stupidly young. "Nothing could change my feelings for Heath."

"Nothing?" Simon said. Then he walked away mumbling under his breath, "I'll have to remind you of that."

But Adrien knew he would never need reminding. His life was perfect.

Nothing could shake his happiness.

# PART THREE

## Birth and Afterbirth

# Chapter Eighteen

"WHICH OF YOU plan to raise the child? Or do you plan to raise the child together?" Heath read aloud from the book, his voice almost shaking with anxiety. His forehead and the small of his back broke out into a sweat, and he held his breath to keep from begging Adrien to stay here with him forever.

"I..." Adrien glanced up at him, as if trying to read his face.

Heath gazed back down at him as carefully neutral as possible. "What would you like, Adrien?"

"What are my options?" Adrien asked.

Heath read the question again, "Which of you plan to raise the child? Or do you plan to raise the child together?"

"No, I mean, could I take my baby with me? Or..." He cleared his throat, gazing down, his neck turning red.

Heath's heart went off like a bang. He heaved in a panicked breath. "No," he said firmly. "You could not take the child with you."

Adrien fluttered his lashes, his cheeks going pale. "So if I left here, I'd go alone. Would I be allowed to see him again?"

Heath swallowed hard. His mind whirred, and he rubbed at his forehead. Already this was going all wrong. Adrien was supposed to have said, "I want to raise him together," and Heath was supposed to say, "I want that, too," but now Adrien was talking about taking the baby or having visitation rights. Fuck!

"You would be allowed to see him," Heath gritted out.

"But..."

"But?"

"But that's not what I want to happen."

"You don't want me to see him?" Adrien's eyes went wide with hurt. He reached for his glasses on the table by the bed and put them on.

"No! I mean...yes, I want you to see him." Heath took Adrien's chin in his hands and tilted his head up, gazing at his eyes through the glasses lenses. "I don't want you to leave him—or me—at all."

Adrien's smile was the sweet, helpless, silly one that made Heath's gut do somersaults. "Yeah?"

"Yeah."

"So how would that work? Exactly?"

"You'd stay here."

"In the nest?"

"No. I imagine once the wee one is a few weeks old, you'll want to get out and explore. And when he's a bit older, you'll want to make a life of some kind. Return to school or take on charity work of some kind. Until you get pregnant again."

Adrien's smile was like sunshine in spring. Sweet, uplifting, perfect. Heath never felt more alpha than when that smile was turned his way. "You want to do this with me again?" Adrien said, touching his stomach. It shifted restlessly beneath his hand. "But you haven't even met him yet. What if he's not what you were expecting?"

"He'll be yours and mine, and that's what I've wanted from the beginning."

Adrien rubbed his stomach, his joyful expression almost painfully sweet. "That's what I want, too," he said finally. "That's what I've wanted for a long time now."

Heath's heart exploded with elation. "So you'll stay?"

"I'll stay."

"And you'll raise him with me?"

"I don't want to leave him the way my omega parent left me. I want to be there for him." Adrien took Heath's hand with a touching laugh. "I saw those pictures in your album of you and your omega parent, your da, and I felt for the first time how much I wish I'd known mine. Heard his laugh. Known his voice. I don't want my child to grow up without that. Even though I know you'd take good care of him. You and Simon."

"Simon's too old to be his nurse. We'll need to hire a new one."

"Simon will be his grandfather," Adrien said firmly.

"Essentially, I suppose he will." Heath kissed Adrien's nose and removed his glasses again, putting them on the nightstand. "I need you on my cock now," he rasped. "Where you belong."

Adrien didn't hesitate, straddling his hips and sliding down onto Heath's cock with ease. He was wet and clingy on the inside, and it drove Heath wild to watch him writhe on his cock, his pregnant stomach so taut and hard, and his dick jutting out from beneath it with pink urgency.

"That's it," he said as Adrien worked himself up to a frenzy. "You belong right here. With me. Riding my cock."

"Yes," Adrien agreed, his chest, throat, and cheeks red, and his cock dripping pre-cum all over Heath's furry stomach. "Yes, I belong with you."

"Belong *to* me," Heath corrected.

And Adrien didn't hesitate to agree. "Yes. I belong to you. I'm yours." He put one hand over the bulge of his stomach and groaned, "We're yours."

"Fuck, yes," Heath shouted, gripping Adrien's hips and plowing up into him hard and fast. He loved fucking this boy, loved his noises and his body. Loved knowing that his child was planted inside, growing so fast, and going to be born so soon. He loved the way milk leaked from Adrien's nipples, slipping down his sweaty chest and sliding down his stomach. He loved the way Adrien didn't care anymore, didn't question it. He was the most accepting, beautiful, delicious man he'd ever met, and he wanted to fuck him until the end of time.

That was his last thought before orgasm took him. He crowed, arching up, fucking deeply into Adrien's squirming body, and reveled in the rapid-fire spurts of cum that shot from Adrien's dick. He shuddered and groaned, filling up Adrien's ass with his semen, eyes rolling back, as he gritted his teeth and rode out the shocks of ecstasy that were almost too much, too good.

He was just coming down from that high when he felt the heat of slick gushing over his stomach, hips, and thighs. Copious slick. Like a water balloon had burst over his groin and body.

Adrien was still coming, his body shaking as he spurted load after load, but Heath stared up in shock as more slick—no, fluid—poured from Adrien's ass. He waited until Adrien was done coming, and then pulled him down, until they were resting on their sides. He was still deep in Adrien, enjoying his heat and tightness, as he waited for Adrien to calm down enough to notice.

Eventually, he did, but not until his entire abdomen went tight and hard and he groaned in pain. "Oh!" he cried out. "Did we… I think we hurt the baby!"

"No," Heath said calmly, stroking Adrien's cheek. "You've gone into labor. A little early. But not too early. The doctor said it could be anytime now, remember?"

Adrien's eyes went wide.

Heath felt strong tension around his cock as another labor pain gripped Adrien. When it had passed, Heath pulled out slowly. Another gush of fluid pulsed out of Adrien's ass, along with actual slick this time. His body's way of lubricating the baby's exit. They'd read about this part just a few weeks before in the pregnancy book.

Time flashed in and out of Heath's mind.

Later, he remembered yelling for Simon to call the doctor, and he remembered Adrien's face distorted in agony. He remembered blood, and Adrien's hand clenching his so hard that he thought his bones would break. He remembered a lot of things, but none so clearly as the moment his child—their child—burst out of Adrien's body like a canon shot.

The doctor caught him, covered in white stickiness and gore, and wiped him down quickly, before passing him up to Adrien, who reached for him immediately. Heath's chest felt almost too full for breath, and then he realized why. He was crying.

"I love you," Adrien whispered to the baby, kissing his still-damp, screaming head. "I love you so much."

Heath cuddled them both close, burying his face in Adrien's neck, and tried to stifle the sobs. He didn't know what was wrong with him. Seeing his child had undone something inside him, and he couldn't get it tied up tight again. Adrien cooed and soothed, and Heath didn't know if it was for him or the baby.

Probably for both.

He kissed Adrien's shoulder and hastily wiped at his eyes, sitting up to get a better look at his son.

ADRIEN HADN'T EVER felt pain like that before. And he wasn't sure he ever wanted to feel pain like that again.

Though staring down at his son, sucking hungrily at his chest, eating for the first time, he thought it might, possibly, be worth it.

The doctor had seen him through it all and then promptly

disappeared with a hearty congratulations for them both. Simon had hovered outside the door, and they'd let him in once the doctor had left. He paced now in urgent excitement, his jowls shaking with each step, and his voice high-pitched with joy. "He's beautiful, lovey. He's perfect. What will you name him?"

"Calm down, old man, or you'll give yourself a heart attack," Heath muttered, though his eyes remained suspiciously wet.

Adrien had been in too big of a state of shock—what with an infant having just shot out of his asshole—to really absorb it earlier, but he was starting to feel it now: Heath had been so moved that he'd *cried*. Good God, they were both ridiculous. And in love. And now in love with this baby, too.

Adrien's heart soared. He'd never known such happiness could exist. How could his omega parent have walked away from this? Sure, his father hadn't been like Heath, but he'd been a good man, and…

He cut his thoughts off. That didn't matter. He and Heath would raise this baby together. They'd make more. They'd never part. It was bliss of the highest order, and the only sad thing in the world was that not everyone was lucky enough to experience it.

He'd have to call Ron Finch and thank him for setting up the auction, for encouraging the breeding option, and for making him sound so appealing in the write-up. It was absurd to contemplate that had it not been for all of that he would be at university right now thinking about Hontu fabric and not holding his baby son.

Thank God Heath had won him!

"Yes, yes," Simon said, making an obvious effort to calm down. He approached the bed again and stared down at where the baby was latched on, gobbling away, his little mouth and cheeks moving adorably. "He's handsome. Looks like you both."

"Does he?" Adrien put his glasses on so he could see his son a bit better. "I think he looks like Heath."

"Dark hair, same skin tone," Heath said agreeably. "But that nose and chin are all you."

"Maybe. He's so scrunched up. How can we really tell?"

Simon reached out a single finger and smoothed it over the baby's thatch of dark hair. "He's wondrous."

"And you thought it was a bad idea," Heath grumbled.

"I did not!" Simon protested. "I thought the plan was a bad idea…" He trailed off, glancing at Adrien and then back at the baby again. "No matter. I was wrong. This little miracle was a wonderful idea."

"But you posed a good question," Heath said. "What should we call him?"

Adrien's stomach flip-flopped, and he gathered his nerve to make his suggestion.

"Yes?" Heath encouraged him. "I can see you have something in mind."

"I think we should call him Nathan, after the man you loved? The one who died?"

Simon gasped.

Heath jerked back as if slapped. His face turned red, and his breath came in short gasps. "No. Choose something else."

Adrien blinked up at him, an ache in his gut where moments ago only joy had been. "I'm sorry. I thought you'd like it."

"I do." Heath shook his head, wiped his hand over his mouth, and said, "Just pick something else."

Simon stepped away from the bed, as though he wanted to make himself invisible. Adrien's chest hurt. He didn't know what he'd done wrong.

"Michael? After my father, then?"

Heath nodded. "That's good. I like it."

Adrien fought back the lump in his throat and peered down at his son. How could he be hurt when his child was perfect, plump, and snuggled in so tight against him chestfeeding? His glasses fogged from the puff of his own hot breath and the humidity of the suddenly hot room. He took them off again.

It was fine. They were fine.

Michael it would be, and it was a good name.

"Michael," he said aloud, testing it.

"He was an angel," Simon offered as he left. "One of God's finest."

Heath swallowed hard and seemed to make an effort to soften at Adrien's side in the bed. "Yes, Michael. The angel of triumph."

The tension in the room dissolved, and eventually Adrien fell asleep. When he woke, the room was dark, but Michael and Heath were nestled up beside him, and he checked the baby for his breath. Upon finding it steady and strong, he slipped off back into dreams.

# Chapter Nineteen

TO ADRIEN'S EYES, Heath seemed happier than ever, perhaps even deliriously so, after the baby's birth. He smiled constantly and was a helpful, adoring father to Michael and devoted alpha to Adrien.

But it wasn't the same for Adrien. As the first few days passed, he grew restless, tired, and anxious. His skin didn't hurt like it did before, but he felt like his insides had taken over the job of aching. He couldn't use the bathroom without pain, and while he knew that was normal, it stressed him out. He didn't want to eat because that meant he'd later have to endure the bathroom agony, but if he didn't eat then Michael wouldn't get the right nutrients, and he just wanted to sleep, dammit, but Michael wanted to chestfeed, and it was harder than he'd thought.

He wanted that rosy glow back. The one he'd carried through his whole pregnancy. The one that had fallen over him like a protective blanket up until the birth, whispering to him that everything was all right.

Instead, he had a weird, nagging feeling that everything was all wrong. And he had no idea how to settle it. He straightened his glasses as he paced with a fussing Michael up and down the long hallway. It no longer felt magical. He felt like he knew every nub and dent in the concrete.

"It's the hormone drop," Heath said calmly, falling into step next to him. He reached out to rub Adrien's neck, but that felt condescending, and Adrien shrugged him off. "You've been riding the pregnancy hormones for months, and getting plenty of my semen, too, which has a calming effect. Now, you haven't been taking in any since the birth. I could jerk off into your mouth. That might help."

Adrien glared at him. He was tired, upset, and couldn't take a shit without thinking he was going to die, but Heath wanted to jerk off into his mouth? Fuck him.

"No."

"It might help."

"No."

"I could put some in a glass for you then. You could drink it like milk."

Adrien gazed down at Michael's frowning face and sighed. "All right."

"I'll leave it for you in the fridge."

Adrien turned up a lip. "Cold jizz. Thanks. Delicious."

"I can give it to you warm. I already offered."

"No!" Adrien kissed Michael's fat baby cheeks, wishing he didn't feel so growly inside. He was being unfair to Heath. He headed back down the tunnel into the living room of the nest again. "I don't like the idea of Simon seeing it in the refrigerator."

"This is common," Heath said, following him. "Everyone knows omegas can go through this. Post-partum drop. It's normal."

"It's not normal! It's awful!"

Heath took Michael from him. "Why don't you try to get some sleep? I'll take care of this little booger."

Adrien thought about arguing. He hated being away from Michael for even a few minutes. It felt wrong that the little being who'd so recently been inside him could ever be more than a hand's reach away.

"I'll just rest here on the couch." He lay down on his side and grabbed a throw pillow to cling to. He watched Heath sit with Michael in the rocking chair Simon had brought down from somewhere in the big house. Heath hummed, his deep voice vibrating through Adrien soothingly.

He relaxed. Okay, this was all right. Good, even. He took off his glasses and put them on the arm of the sofa. When he woke up, he'd be over whatever was happening, whatever nastiness was growing in his head. He'd go back to feeling that lovely peace and contentment he'd felt before.

But when he did wake, he felt no different. Plus, Heath was gone, and Michael was in Simon's arms in the garden. He tightened his robe, wondering when he'd be able to fit in his old clothes, put on his glasses, and stepped outside. He frowned. The roses had started to fade over the last few days.

"Autumn's coming on," Simon said, answering his unspoken question. "Won't be long until the bushes are bare. But they come back new every year." He kissed Michael's little head and smiled at Adrien, his old eyes crinkling at the edges. "Heath left something in the refrigerator for you. He said you should have it right away."

Adrien gritted his teeth. He did miss the taste of Heath's cum. He missed the feeling of him pumping it deep into his ass the most, but that particular orifice felt like it would never be the same again.

A new fear dug its claws in.

What if it *was* never the same? What if Heath didn't want him anymore?

A spike of anger shot through him.

Heath had bought his heat, bred him, and pampered him. Told him he loved him. He'd let him believe that they could be happy together. What was wrong with Adrien to be so suspicious now? Why was he so upset?

"Drink what Heath left for you, lad," Simon said kindly. "You'll feel better for it."

Adrien took Michael from him. "He needs to eat," he said, though the baby usually fussed when he was hungry. He took him into the gazebo and sat on the bench, undoing his robe enough to feed him. He looked out over the garden with renewed interest. He hadn't worn his glasses so often when he was pregnant, and everything looked crisper through the lenses.

What would winter look like from his nest? No green leafy trees in the forest outside his room. No red roses in the garden. No sweet scents slipping into his nose lulling him into peace. Winter would be gray and cold. Different. Stark.

Adrien wondered if he'd stay to see it.

HEATH PACED HIS office.

Adrien wasn't doing well at all since the birth. He'd called the doctor twice and been told both times that this behavior was normal. Almost all omegas experienced hormone drop after birth. He was instructed to feed him alpha cum as often as possible and wait it out.

But there was something wrong. Heath sensed it.

Or maybe it was the guilt in his gut turning over and over.

There was so much he had kept from Adrien, so much that he needed to tell him.

Not to mention, he had a child now—an alpha child at that—and thus an obligation to inform his brother, Lidell, and his nephew, Ned, that he had a new heir. That was going to be an ugly conversation. Not helped any by the last interaction he'd had with them, before Adrien had been close to birthing Michael.

Ned had been caught in an orgy again. Not a big deal in the scheme of life, except for the fact that, in the basement where this orgy was held, an omega had been gagged, tied to the bed, beaten with whips, and fucked against his will.

That was rape, and while Ned swore that he'd had nothing to do with it, hadn't even known it was happening, and that he'd been taking part with willing—*happily* willing, he'd insisted—omegas upstairs, the amount of work Heath had needed to put in to protect the family's reputation, and Ned's, was immense. Because, God help him, he believed his nephew was a lazy, lustful sod, but he wasn't a rapist.

Still, he'd told Lidell off for not keeping a better leash on Ned, and, as usual, that'd led to all kinds of bad blood being brought to the surface. "So says the brother that I literally had to peel off omegas when he was in college."

"I was a worthless pig, but that doesn't mean Ned should be."

"Then you took up with that trash!"

"Don't talk about Nathan. He's dead. Show some respect."

"Respect? For the low-class user who wanted your money and nothing more? He fucked how many alphas behind your back? Probably in your own bed! He even let one breed him, for fuck's sake. Thank all that's holy the pregnancy didn't take because you would have raised that bastard as your own and put him in as heir."

"Shut your foul mouth," Heath had shouted, his hand going around his brother's throat. He'd shoved him against the wall and shaken him. It hadn't been nice. It hadn't been kind. It definitely hadn't been pretty. It'd echoed all their interactions since childhood: Lidell needling him until he used the threat of violence to shut him up.

It was a side of himself he didn't like. A side of himself that Nathan had only seen once. During that very episode Lidell had the nerve to bring up. The baby hadn't lingered in Nathan's womb; it was true. But it wasn't because of Heath. Lidell told it true. Heath would have raised it as his own if it meant that Nathan would stay. But instead, Nathan had gone off alone for a week and come back saying it had been taken care of, and that, strangely enough, had hurt Heath almost more than the infidelity that had brought the baby into their lives.

He sat down at his desk, rubbing his face with his hand. He hadn't shaved since Michael was born. He hadn't intended to let his beard come back in, but it was, relentless and dark.

Like him, he supposed.

He picked up the phone to make the call. Now was as good a time as ever.

Might as well bring at least a few secrets into the light.

# Chapter Twenty

FOR THE FIRST time in a long time, Adrien remembered he had a cell phone. He plugged it into the wall and let it charge, surprised when a number of texts came through and a lot of missed-call notifications. He scanned through the alerts and was touched to see that Lance had sent most of them. His research team at the university, and even Ron Finch, had all messaged multiple times to check on his progress and health, too. They must have thought he was a total asshole to have never responded.

He used the phone to take a picture of himself with Michael and sent it to Lance and the others with a short message.

*Announcing the birth of Michael Clearwater. 6lbs 4oz. Healthy and doing well. Thank you all for your kindness during my pregnancy. It was appreciated.*

Then he sent another message just to Lance.

*Sorry I missed your calls and texts. I forgot to charge my phone for a few months. Pregnancy hormones will do that to a guy. Thanks for trying to keep in touch. I'll do better.*

A short time later his phone rang. And for the first time since he'd arrived at Heath's house, he spoke to someone outside of his nest.

"So what's his place like? Amazing?"

"I've stayed in the nest most of the time."

"The nest?"

"Yeah, these really comfortable rooms and a garden that he had made for me." It wasn't true that they'd been made *for him*, but he'd pretended long enough that it felt true, and it made him feel special to say so. Lance didn't know the difference. "I actually haven't ever left it."

"Wow. So you have no clue what the rest of his pad is like?"

"It's a castle," Adrien said, laughing softly. "I saw some of it when I first arrived. It was imposing."

"You're living in a castle, but you haven't gone exploring? Are you even allowed to or is this some Bluebeard kind of shit?"

"Bluebeard…?"Adrien didn't get the reference.

"Right. I forgot about your weird religious background. It's an old fairytale about an older alpha who breeds a young omega. They're happy. In love. But he tells the omega the one thing he must never do is look inside this one room."

Adrien felt a weird chill go up his back. He thought irrationally of the photo album with Nathan's name on it. "And?"

"So of course the omega looked in the room one day."

"And?" God, why was Lance making him work for this? He already felt sick to his stomach as it was. Probably from the hormone letdown, but…but…there was something else, too.

"It was full of the bones of all the dead omegas he'd bred before him. He'd killed them. The babies, too. Supposedly for daring to look in the room? Or maybe it was because he was insane?"

"Because killing people for looking in a room *isn't* insane?"

"Maybe they died in childbirth. I don't know. But in the end of the version my omega parent told me, the omega ran for his life and never looked back. But I read a version here at university where he was caught looking in the room, and his alpha killed him and his baby, too."

Adrien shuddered, holding baby Michael closer. "Good story, friend," he said, mimicking the way Lance always talked to him. "Hilarious."

"I'm not saying your man's gonna murder you," Lance said slowly. "But I'm just asking why you're not allowed to look around."

"I am allowed. I just haven't."

"Why?"

"Wait until you're knocked up. Then you'll understand."

"The nudity thing?" Lance said, scoffing. "Please. I have no shame. I'll be naked as a jaybird everywhere and anywhere I want in my alpha's house. Everyone can just deal with it. My youngest step-omega parent was always naked. He just gave up clothes eventually. My father liked it that way."

"I bet he did." Adrien sighed. He almost regretted talking to Lance now. He already missed the blissful bubble he'd lived in while growing Michael so much, and with every word, Lance was destroying it even more.

At that moment, Michael started to fuss, which gave Adrien the perfect excuse to disconnect the call after promising not to drop off the face of the earth again. He opened his robe, grateful that his skin was no longer so sensitive that even the silk felt harsh, and placed Michael onto his nipple.

The sharp pain of Michael latching on reminded him of Heath's pinching fingers when they'd fucked, and he felt a strong, overwhelming loss at the memory. He shoved that thought out of his mind.

He cuddled Michael close, watching his fat cheeks move as he suckled, and marveled at the hot gushes of milk he felt spurt out of his nipple. It was remarkable how much his chest could hold. He knew some omegas grew much larger, but he'd remained relatively flat. Still Michael never seemed to run out of nourishment from his body.

He lay back in bed with Michael and fed him. He stared out the windows into the glowing green of the forest, noticing that some of the leaves were turning yellow, others orange, and one, very deep in the trees, was edged with red.

A shudder rocked him.

He didn't want to be in this room when the leaves fell. The rest of the castle was a mystery, and he didn't know if there was another room within it that he could bear to sleep in, but his blood ran cold at the thought of staying in this room during winter. The forest cold, the trees barren, and the skies a dull gray.

When Michael fell asleep, he made up his mind. He got out of bed, washed in the shower, and put on some of his old clothes. The fabric felt rough against his skin, and the waist was tight enough that he couldn't button his pants closed, but he pulled his shirt down over it and left them open at the top. Finally, he put his glasses on, then he lifted Michael into his arms and stepped out of the room.

He heard Simon singing in the kitchen. He considered going to him and asking for a tour, but then he remembered that photo album. Simon had brought it to him. He'd wanted him to know about whatever—whoever—was inside. But something about that felt sinister now.

It was probably the hormone drop making him paranoid.

But if it wasn't… Didn't he deserve to know? He had Michael to think of now. What kind of man was Heath beyond the door of the nest? What was he hiding?

Adrien turned toward the door he'd entered by all those months ago, gripped Michael tightly, and walked through.

HEATH STARED AT his brother. He couldn't believe the man had driven in from the seaside to have it out with him over something that was a done deal.

"The child is born. He's mine. What's done is done," Heath said again.

"You did this on purpose!" Lidell spit out, pointing his finger at Heath, neck red with rage.

Heath huffed a laugh. "Yes, I did. I bought an omega's heat, bred him, and knocked him up *on purpose*. And I had every right to do so."

"Not just any omega," Lidell said under his breath, a sneer twisting his mouth.

Heath knew just where that rumor had come from. "Earl should keep his mouth shut," Heath spit out. "When I allowed him to stay on as Ned's nurse and then his servant, it was with the understanding that anything Simon told him at home was private."

"When it comes to protecting his charge, Earl knows where his loyalties lie!" Lidell said. "He puts Ned first. Unlike some people."

Heath blinked at his brother. "Why on earth would I put Ned first?"

"Because he's your heir!"

"Was my heir." Heath rolled his eyes. "Ned! Come in here."

The young man peeked his head around the doorway outside of Heath's office, where he'd been charged with waiting while Heath spoke with Lidell privately. He stepped in, his cheeks flushed, anger flashing in his eyes, but a kind of puffiness in the mouth, too, like he'd been chewing his lip so that he wouldn't cry.

"Ned," Heath said less harshly. "You won't be without a large fortune settled on you. To be honest, you probably won't even notice the difference in the functionality of your life. Except, of course, that you won't have to worry about ever taking over for me here."

"Unless something happens to the brat," Lidell said.

Heath roared, and Lidell hustled back toward the leather sofa near a sidewall. "You can't hurt me!" he cried. "Ned is a witness."

"If you threaten my child—"

"It wasn't a threat!" Lidell exclaimed, pale and cowering. "It wasn't a threat, Heath. I promise."

Heath calmed himself, embarrassed to find spittle on his beard from the force of his shouts. He wiped it off with the back of his hand and turned to face the window.

"Ned, you'll be fine. You'll be wealthy and handsome. You'll have your pick of omegas when it comes time to negotiate, or you can afford to have one at auction if that's more your speed."

"You plan to just discard him, then?"

"This is hardly discarding him, Lidell. I'm setting him up for life. Just like I did for you."

"Our father did that."

"And I let him," Heath countered. "If I'd really wanted to put the nails to you, brother, I could have convinced him to leave every cent to me, and you know it." Heath smoothed a hand over his beard. "Instead, you've had houses in the best areas, sent your son to the best schools, had my help in bailing him out of all sorts of unfortunate circumstances, and lived in leisure. I've never understood why you saw fit to complain."

"Because you get everything good."

"The stress? The strain? The worry? Carrying on our family reputation, keeping up our business interests, finding more, making sure our properties and interests stay sound, caring for the servants? That's the good stuff you're so jealous of?"

"You have purpose at least. Now you're going to strip my boy of that."

"You can design your own purpose, Lidell. How many times have I told you to go find something you love and do it well? But you whine and fuss. You could have started your own dynasty by now, but you've pissed it all away in legal fees trying to find ways to declare me unfit."

"That slut you carried on with should have been more than enough reason," Lidell hissed. "Sleeping his way through all of your business associates. You know he affected your decision making, and he still does."

"Shut your mouth."

"Nathan was your undoing. And now you've gone and—"

"I said, shut your fucking mouth!"

Lidell slammed his lips together, but then Ned took up the cause.

"My whole life you said I was gonna be the master of this place, that I was going to be the Clearwater heir. You said I had to take care to be a good man because of it. Now you say I'm not!"

"If you've been acting the part of a 'good man,' Ned, then I am terrified to know what you would have done without that incentive."

"That's right!" Ned said, nodding and crossing his arms over his chest. "You're taking away my motivation. Now, what'll I be? Nothing good!"

Heath rolled his eyes and threw up his hands. "The devil take you both."

A small sound from the doorway drew his attention, and when his eyes met Adrien's, at first his heart leapt, and then it fell.

# Chapter Twenty-One

THE HOUSE WAS a maze, truly, and there weren't many servants around as far as Adrien could see. At least, he didn't run into any as he walked from room to lavish room, goggling at the monstrosity of riches nearly frothing from every corner.

This was the least Heath-like home he could imagine. Or maybe he didn't know Heath at all.

The cold feeling he hated slid over him again. He kissed Michael's head and pressed on into the house, looking for what, he didn't know. He thought he'd understand when he found it, or maybe he was finally getting to see the real Heath. The one the world knew.

Imposing. Scary. Dominating.

The Heath who'd asked to see his asshole and made him lick his cum off his boot in front of the heat cabin.

Raised voices came from a room near the back of the 'castle.' He made out Heath's tones and two other men. It sounded heated, and he knew he should turn back, but he didn't.

He walked silently on his bare feet down the hallway, the sensation of clothes against his skin uncomfortable after months without them. He stopped in the doorway to a large office with views of the front drive and the park going off into the distance.

"The devil take you both!" Heath exclaimed, throwing his hands up in the air. His dark eyes glittered dangerously above his beard. His eyes landed on Adrien then, and they softened.

"Adrien? What are you doing up here?"

The two men beside Heath turned to face him, and immediately one of them scoffed. The other, younger one simply looked confused—angry, still, but confused. "You seriously did it, didn't you?" the older man said. "You got his son. I'd heard the rumor, but I didn't actually believe it."

Heath's eyes hardened as he swung his attention back to the men in the room.

"You bred your lover's son? That's demented!" the younger one said, a snarl of disgust on his lips.

"My lover, not my husband," Heath corrected, though his eyes were back on Adrien, who felt like a ghost—tingly and unreal, floating outside of his body. "We were never married."

"You fucked him enough to be married," the elder said.

"Shut up, Lidell!" Heath snarled, his fists clenching. He took a step toward his brother like he was going to hit him, and Lidell took a step back, his face blanching.

"Calm down," Lidell said, putting up his hands. "I just hadn't thought you were still so cock-smitten that you'd go this far to get a piece of him back."

Ned, because Adrien knew now that the younger man must be Lidell's son, the troublemaker and former heir, turned to him and stared in utter rage. "You! You stole my inheritance!" he shouted, starting forward with his fists clenched.

Heath grabbed Ned by his shirt neck and hauled him back. "Touch him, and you'll be more than disinherited. You'll be dead."

Adrien cradled Michael close to his thundering heart. "I'll go."

"No, you should stay." Heath's brother snarled at him. "We're the ones who should go."

Michael squirmed in his arms, and Adrien bounced him

softly. "I was exploring."

"So I see," Heath said a little grimly, but then he smiled softly and added, "I'm being rude. This is my brother, Lidell Clearwater, and his son, Ned. They're here to learn more about the changes in the entail to the estate since Michael came along."

"Did Nathan put you up to this?" Lidell asked Adrien, not putting out a hand or acting at all interested in polite introductions. "Did he convince *you* to take up his cause of messing up Heath's life?"

"Nathan?" Adrien asked, knowing full well they were referring to the man Heath had loved and lost. The mystery man who had slipped into his thoughts relentlessly ever since Heath had reacted so badly to the name suggestion.

"Yes. Your omega parent! Nathan!" Lidell said, and then he cowered as Heath strode across the room, grabbed him by the arm, and dragged him toward the door.

"Excuse us, Adrien. My brother's overstayed his welcome." He called over his shoulder, "You, too, Ned."

The sullen teen followed Heath and Lidell out of the room. Adrien stood by the doorway, out of arm's reach, with Michael held close, like they were predators of some sort.

His head ached. His body throbbed. He felt nauseous. What had Lidell meant by saying Nathan was his omega parent? Or that Heath had bred his lover's son?

He felt a little faint. He hadn't eaten enough, and he was dizzy. He found the edge of the sofa the Ned boy had been sitting on and dropped down onto it. He lifted his shirt and latched Michael on. Adrien listened to his greedy gulps and waited for the calming hit of the chestfeeding hormones to come. They weren't as good as the pregnancy hormones or the effect of consuming alpha cum, but it was still a nice dose of calmness to keep him from running screaming into the park.

"Are you all right?" Heath asked, coming back in with a worried gleam in his eye and a disheveled look to his clothing, like there'd been a tussle. "My brother oversteps. He always does. Don't be upset that he treated you rudely. He's a snob."

"Why did he say that?"

"What?" Heath said, but his eyes glinting above the darkness of his beard were cagey.

"About Nathan. That he was my omega parent."

"My brother's upset about—"

Adrien straightened his glasses and peered at Heath. "Is it true?"

Heath rubbed his hand over his beard, and Adrien couldn't help but think of Lance's story of Bluebeard. What had he done? Who had he sold himself to? Whose son had he born?

"Did you kill Nathan?" he asked quietly, his worst unconscious fear rising to the surface.

Heath startled. "Little one, that's absurd. I loved Nathan."

"Don't call me that."

"I—"

"I want to know the truth, Heath. And I want to know it now." Michael gobbled hungrily at his chest, and tears welled in Adrien's eyes. He hated it.

"Let's go back down to the nest. I'll call for Simon," Heath said slowly. "So we can talk without Michael."

THE BLUE LEATHER book with the white card sat in his lap.

*Nathan.*

Adrien ran his fingers over the letters. "I never knew my omega father's name. The records were sealed from me."

"Nathan Battershell. He was..." Heath trailed off.

"So that's why you used that name in the auction?" Adrien's throat hurt from holding back tears. "You're telling me that my omega parent was your lover? That this book is full of pictures of him?"

"Yes, that's right."

Adrien's chin quivered. "I hate you so much right now. I'm hurt. Angry. I want to kick you and bite you and hurt you back." He wiped his eyes. "But part of me wants to thank you because this…" He tapped the book. "Is something I've wanted to know for so long."

Heath touched the back of Adrien's neck, sliding his hand up as though to trail into his hair.

Adrien hissed and knocked it away. "Don't touch me again unless you want me to fight you."

"You wouldn't win, little one."

"I don't care. I'd leave marks." He felt scarred inside and out already.

Heath nodded, his eyes downcast and full of shame. "Will you ever forgive me?"

"I don't know right now." Adrien's fingers clenched the edges of the photo album.

"Do you want me to go?"

Adrien hesitated. Part of him wanted to be alone to look at the pictures, to see his omega parent for the first time. But another part of him wanted to know more. Wanted to understand the pictures, to understand why Nathan was smiling or laughing, to know where he was and what he was doing when each shot was taken.

"No," he said. "Stay."

Heath sat very still and didn't argue.

Adrien opened the book.

The first picture was in color. He didn't know why he'd expected it to be in black and white like the pictures in Heath's baby album, but he had. Instead, he was greeted by a sharp smile, laughing eyes, and a face remarkably like his own. But *more* somehow. Like Adrien was just an echo of a complicated but stunning song.

Nathan was handsome. No, *dashing*.

He turned the pages slowly, questions heavy on this tongue. Too heavy to actually speak them.

Every picture revealed a confidence that Adrien had always lacked. Nathan's casual, languid poses, his mischievous gaze, and a certainty in his expression that whoever was behind the camera—Heath, it had to be—was absolutely besotted with him. And yet there was an edge of cruelty in the set of Nathan's mouth and the slant of his stare. Like he knew he could hurt Heath and get away with it. Like he knew that he could and he had.

No, he *did*.

Adrien's hand trembled as he turned another page and another. Fashionable clothes. Fancy yachts. Mountain lodges. Tuxedos. Photos with Heath. Photos alone. Photos of Nathan nude. Photos of him posed. Casual photos and professional ones, too.

Pages of pictures of a man Adrien could never know, or love, or understand. A man Heath had loved before Adrien—did he even love him? Or was he just a piece of Nathan that Heath had managed to scavenge? Like Lidell and Ned had implied?

"Why did you love him?" Adrien finally asked, lingering on a photo of Nathan with his head tossed back, laughter creasing his handsome face, and a glass of champagne held loosely in his hand. He was standing by another alpha, a tall, dark man with wide hands, who had them all over Nathan's hips. Adrien wondered how Heath had felt about that then. How he felt about it now.

"He was an asshole," Heath said sadly. "A beautiful, cruel

asshole."

"That's the kind of man you love?"

"No. I love you, and you're kind, gentle, trusting. Nathan was never trusting."

"Maybe I shouldn't have been either," Adrien spit out, shooting Heath a dark glare.

"I didn't mean to hurt you. When I—"

"I don't want your excuses again. I want the truth. Why did you love him?"

"Because he was—" Heath waved at the album. "I was bewitched."

"And when you bought my heat, it was to have a piece of him?"

"Yes."

"And when you fucked me in the heat cabin, you wanted to knock me up because I was Nathan's son."

Heath swallowed, a confused expression flitting over his face. "At first."

"When I came here, did you want me here because I was Nathan's son or—"

"No! That's not why I wanted you here."

"Why not?"

"At the cabin. That's when it changed for me."

"While we were fucking," Adrien said acidly.

"Yes. No. Just there. In the cabin with you."

He'd never heard Heath sound so lost. "So why didn't you tell me then?"

"What was I supposed to say? You were scared and needed me to guide you. Was I supposed to tell you while you were out of your mind in heat, 'By the way, I fucked your omega parent years ago, but now he's dead, and I'm hoping you can bring part of him back to me'?"

Adrien's throat tightened. He couldn't breathe. He bent his head over the photo album, the scent of the old pages filling his nostrils, and he choked on it as a tear splattered next to the picture of Nathan laughing.

"He wasn't kind," Heath said. "He was unfaithful and drove me mad. He was like a drug to me."

"Like you've been a drug to me."

"I hope not. You've made me feel complete. He made me nuts," Heath said. "Our lovemaking was violent and consuming. But while you were pregnant, what we shared kept you calm, brought you joy. It's not the same."

"So with him, my omega parent—*Nathan*." Oh, how that name tasted bitter in his mouth; thank God Heath hadn't agreed to it for Michael. "With him, it was the thrill of the chase."

Heath rubbed at his forehead. "Nathan would give himself to me completely. I'd feel high, wild with joy. Then he'd pull away from me. Say he needed time alone. Go off with another alpha. I'd go insane." Heath squeezed his eyes shut. "Then he'd come back to me. I'd be angry at first, but he'd flash his smile. He'd take off his clothes. Promise to make a child with me during his next heat." Heath swallowed thickly. "It's shameful how I let him treat me."

"But you loved it."

Heath shook his head. "It was an obsession. I see that now."

"And I'm part of that obsession. Michael and me."

"No! You and Michael are the best things I've ever done."

"We're just a new obsession. Thanks to Nathan." He wished the name didn't burn to say, but every time it came out of his mouth, it hurt.

"Yes," Heath said, taking the photo album out of Adrien's hands and slamming it shut. "Thanks to Nathan."

Adrien stared in shock as Heath stood up and paced in front

of him, ripping at his hair as he spoke in rapid, angry tones, but clearly meaning every word like fire means to burn.

"It's true! If not for Nathan, we wouldn't be here right now. *Michael* wouldn't be here now." Heath stopped in front of him, glaring down, but his anger hurt more than it intimidated. "If not for Nathan, I wouldn't know what it is to hope for a normal, happy future with a kind man who loves me, or to finally have my feelings for a man returned. I wouldn't know the joy of being a father. Of being your lover and alpha. Of wanting a life with you. I wouldn't have you at all!"

"Because you wouldn't have bid on me."

"Because he gave birth to you!" Heath roared.

Adrien blinked at him.

"He gave birth to you. And, yes, maybe he walked away and left you with your father—who raised you to be the kind of man that Nathan would never have raised you to be. He'd have done the same thing to you that he did to me. You got a clean break from him. That was his gift to you. He didn't torture you for years with promises of love and then yank it away. He let you stay with a man who adored you. So your father was too religious and kept you more innocent than he should have, but he loved you. He had kind eyes. That's what Nathan always said about why he left you with him. 'He had kind eyes.' "

Adrien's chin trembled. His heart ached, and he covered his face with his hands.

"So go on and blame him if you want. Blame *me*. Be angry. But none of what we had—have, could still have—would exist without Nathan. I don't love him anymore. Not just because he's dead. But because he was a cruel man, and he treated me terribly. I understand that now. But I am grateful to him, because he made you, and then I found you, and now we have Michael." He stopped a moment. "And, Adrien, I love you. Our life could be beautiful. Please—" Heath's voice was gruff. "Try to forgive me."

"I want to," Adrien whispered. "I want to forgive you. I'll try. But…"

"But?"

The big clock in the nest ticked as Adrien's mind raced. Finally, he said, "I need to try somewhere else. I can't stay here. In this nest." He looked around the room and it felt exactly like what Heath had denied it was: a comfortable prison.

"So you're going to leave me, too?"

Adrien squeezed his eyes shut. "Maybe. I am Nathan's son after all." He stood, hauling the bag he'd packed while they'd waited for Simon to take Michael over his shoulder. He'd known even then, deep down, what he was going to do. "I'll contact you when Michael and I are settled in. We can arrange for you to visit."

"Where are you taking him?"

"I'll call you when I get there."

Adrien walked toward the door leading to the rest of the castle. Some part of him expected Heath to tackle him, to force him to stay, but he pulled the door open without any effort at all. As he did, he heard Heath roar with pain in the living room. It made his knees weak, but he forced himself forward.

Simon stood outside with Michael in his arms and his cheeks wet with tears.

"You can come visit, too," Adrien said, taking the baby from him. "We'll miss you."

Simon said nothing at all, hiccupping sobs slipping out of his throat.

It wasn't until he'd led Adrien down the winding halls and up the stairs, and then out into the sunlight in front of the massive house that he finally spoke.

"You said nothing could change the way you feel," Simon

rasped. "And I said I'd remind you of that."

Adrien hugged Simon, kissed his soft, wet cheek, and whispered, "I love him. That hasn't changed. But trust… That's another matter."

He climbed into his car that someone had pulled around and left running. There was a baby seat in the back for Michael, and he strapped him in. He looked so small in it, so helpless and tiny. Adrien's heart broke.

He headed down the drive toward the giant gate, his throat tight with screams he couldn't seem to let out.

The fairy tale was over.

# Chapter Twenty-Two

"I DON'T NEED to hear that you told me so."

Heath sat in the gazebo, the empty nest behind him, and plucked the petals from a rose. It had been three days since Adrien left and there had been no word at all. He was trying not to panic, but with every passing minute he imagined all sorts of terrible scenarios. He hadn't slept for more than a few minutes, and he missed them both like his peace depended on them being back in arm's reach.

Simon took the bench across from him and remained silent.

"I should have told him from the start."

Simon shrugged, his jowls shaking with the movement. "You didn't intend to fall for him. How could you have known he'd be so different from Nathan?"

"I was selfish. I didn't see him as his own person until it was too late." Heath plucked the last petal and let it fall. Then turned and snapped off another late bloomer and began to pick it apart, too. "I should have known when the heat crush was so strong."

"And if you had told him then? In the middle of his heat?"

Heath shook his head. "It would have been unfair to him. Forced a choice when he didn't have any. I should have told him before so that he could back out, sell to another alpha."

"I'm not the person you need to be saying all this to, lovey."

Heath groaned. "I hurt him. He trusted me."

"Should have, would have, could have," Simon said, and

tutted. "What's done is done, as you were telling Lidell. Now what are you going to do about it?"

"I wish I knew."

"Moping here isn't going to get your son and lover back."

"I'm not moping," Heath growled.

"What are you doing then? Ignoring the ugly truth again? You screwed up, lovey, and you're going to have to make it right. No amount of sulking and wringing your hands is going to do that. So figure out a plan and enact it. You're Heath Clearwater, heir to the Clearwater estate, and you're in love with a boy who's out of his depth. Go get him."

"What if he doesn't want me to? I've already hurt him enough."

"Heath, for God's sake, he has your son."

"Michael will be safe with him."

"Will he? Adrien is young and has no family, nowhere to go. He's angry with you, and is afraid he can't trust you. He's still in post-partum drop, and he's alone. He needs his alpha." Simon leaned forward, elbows resting on his knees. "And you need him, too. The bond you were building together was a beautiful one. Go claim it."

Heath squeezed the half-destroyed rose in his hand. "I lied to him."

"You didn't lie, you withheld."

Heath huffed. "Are you really going to argue semantics as an excuse, old man? You never let me get away with that as a child."

Simon was silent for a long time then, and Heath thought maybe he was going to stop trying to cajole Heath into action. But alas.

"I remember when Nathan died," Simon said, twisting his hands together in his lap. "After all you'd been through with him, you still grieved him hard. I remember more than one night when you lamented that he had never fully trusted you."

"He didn't."

"Oh, but he did," Simon corrected. "He trusted that you'd always be there for him, no matter what he did, and you were." He shrugged his shoulders and rolled his eyes. "He used you that way, of course, but, Heath, he trusted you completely. He simply wasn't trustworthy *himself*, as evidenced by his broken promises and inability to be honest with you. You're the one who never trusted enough."

Heath snorted. "Excuse me?"

"You never trusted in Nathan's love."

"How could I when he ran around doing whatever he wanted and—"

"Because he always came home to you. Don't get me wrong. Nathan wasn't a good omega for you, but not because he didn't trust you or love you, but because he put you on your knees. He was the one in command. He didn't love you the way you need to be loved—adoringly, unquestioningly, and submissively. The way Adrien does."

Heath ground his teeth, not wanting to hear another word, but pinned in place by the truth. "Did."

Simon ignored his interjection and went on. "You were so afraid that Adrien would be like Nathan that you didn't trust him either. And in his way, he was like his omega parent. From the start, Adrien put his trust in you, like Nathan did. He grew to love you, like Nathan did. But unlike his omega parent, he'd have committed to you, Heath."

"I know what I've lost."

"You're so self-righteous at times, playing the martyr. Oh, brave, honorable Heath, all the other peers say. Helping his horrible brother, supporting his bratty nephew, and putting up with such an unloyal lover." Simon tutted again. "But you're just as much to blame as Lidell, Ned, and Nathan. You take on the savior role like you don't trust that your brother or nephew can handle themselves. You endured Nathan's behavior like you didn't trust in the flow of life to provide you with love. Even now you doubt it, though life has given you love. Twice." Simon spoke firmly. "You always say that Nathan had trust issues, but you're the one with trust issues, Heath."

Heath stared at the man who'd raised him, who'd seen him through it all, good and bad. "What do I do? How do I fix myself? And this?"

"Adrien needs a strong hand."

"Yes."

"In that very important way, he isn't like Nathan. Think of his life, lovey: under his father's command, then under his professor's command at university. He says he wants to be a professor himself, but a *research* professor, a quiet man digging into his particular passions behind the scenes. Adrien complied without question with the matcher at the university. That information was on his auction page. Yes, I looked. Can you ever imagine Nathan doing *that*?"

Simon crossed the gazebo and sat down on the bench next to Heath, putting his wrinkled hand on Heath's knee. "Adrien's good for you in all the ways Nathan never was, because he doesn't put you on your knees. He lets you stand tall and be an alpha. His style of submissive love allows you to feel precious and honored. Those are feelings Nathan never gave you. Every alpha has a weakness, and every omega should know what it is before marrying or making a lifelong commitment. Lack of trust is yours. Adrien knows that now."

"I wish I knew how to shut down my damned heart."

"No, that heart is your greatest gift." Simon squeezed his knee and spoke with great gentleness. "Heath, lovey, he's worth the risk. Adrien isn't running from you because he doesn't care for you, or because he has such a great need for freedom. He's running from you because he didn't know how to stay. Go get him."

"I don't know where he is."

"You do." Simon stood up and stretched. "In your heart, you do. I'm going home to Earl. I'm sure it'll be another night of tales about poor slighted Ned's pity party orgies he's been throwing for the last few days. You Clearwater men, always making things so dramatic."

"I don't know where he's gone," Heath repeated, forlorn, tossing the petals of the destroyed rose to the ground with the others. "You act like I know him, but I don't. We were together for four months and I don't know him at all."

"You're being absurd. I've watched you give him what he needed instinctively the entire time he was here."

"That was sex and hormones, and alpha instincts in reaction to his heat and pregnancy."

Simon put his hands in his pockets. "You know he takes joy in the small things in life: his robe, the tunnel, the garden. He craves comfort, and not just because of the pregnancy. Think of what he said about growing up on the farm: constricted, yes, but he loved the familiarity of it. Think of what he's always studied: fabric, traditional weaving. The comforts of the artistic world."

Heath closed his eyes, imagined Adrien leaving the house, alone and scared with Michael. "He went back to school."

"Of course he did." Simon smiled, his chin wobbling. "You ridiculous fool. Go get him."

With that, Simon walked down the garden path back toward the nest, leaving Heath staring at the litter of petals on the ground, his mind already trying to piece together the right words to say.

*

"I'M JUST LIKE my omega parent," Adrien said miserably,

staring at the pint of hard cider in his hand and wondering if it would be safe to chestfeed Michael if he drank it. He sat at the desk in his dorm room, while Lance sprawled on Adrien's unmade bed.

Lance nudged his fingers. "Drink up. It'll do you some good."

"I don't think I should. Michael…" Adrien straightened his glasses and then gazed at his son, sleeping in a makeshift baby bed made from a cardboard box with a blanket in it on the floor of his dorm room. Heath would be appalled. And maybe he should be.

Adrien gave the pint to Lance. "You drink it."

"Your loss, friend." Lance swallowed down the rest of his own pint and then started on Adrien's. "I'd say you look good except you look fucking miserable."

"I am."

"Good God, why are you here? You should be with your man. Once this little guy is a bit bigger, that's when you come back, for like, day classes, and you take a few extra years to finish up your work."

"I used to care a lot more about my career. I did all this so I could have the funds for the government to agree to name me a professor."

"Babies change things. And you can still be a professor. Your alpha will have plenty of cash to make sure that happens."

"I won't use him like that."

Lance used the empty pint to point at Michael in the cardboard box. "Obviously."

Adrien wiped a hand over his face. "I'm a terrible omega parent."

"No, you're not. You're just dropping from that glorious pregnancy hormone high and crashing hard." Lance shrugged. "I've seen it all before with my step-omega parents."

"This is different."

"How so?"

Adrien didn't know if he had the strength to go into it. He hadn't had a good meal since he found out about Nathan, feeling too sick and hurt at first, and now, spoiled by Simon's cooking, he found the cafeteria food disgusting. Michael still ate a lot, though, and Adrien needed to be careful. Not eating enough while chestfeeding could be dangerous for them both.

"I took him away from his father."

"You can take him back."

"No!"

"I don't mean leave Michael there with him," Lance said gently. "I mean you can go back to your alpha. I know he'd want you." He frowned. "Doesn't he? Or…?"

"He would take us back."

"Then go! This is ridiculous." He pointed at the cardboard box again. "Whatever he did, forgive him and take this baby to a real bed. He's too rich to sleep in a box."

"He's the heir, but I didn't take any money when I left."

"Your auction money—"

"In escrow at the bank until I finish out one year of chestfeeding."

"You are insane. That man could buy and sell this university, and you didn't take anything?"

Adrien shook his head.

Michael squirmed in his cardboard bed and farted.

Lance wrinkled up his nose. "Damn, he's so small. Who knew?" He ran a hand over his fuzzy, dark hair. "I don't know why you're so upset, but I promise unless he's hurting you—holy shit, *is* he hurting you?"

"No."

"Are you sure?"

"Yes, I'm sure." Adrien groaned. "It turns out…" He studied

Lance carefully. "Listen, this is private. I don't want you talking about this with anyone. Heath doesn't need the rumors."

"If you're talking about you being his dead lover's son, then that rumor's done flown, friend."

"What?"

"Yes, everyone knows that. His ex-heir is none too pleased with having been ousted, and he's going around mouthing off about it like there's something illegal about knocking up your dead lover's son. Which there's not. They were never married."

"So everyone here knows?" He thought about the odd looks he'd gotten in the hallway earlier after he'd made his way down to the cafeteria for dinner to push food around on a plate. He'd thought at the time it was because he had Michael with him, but the exact nuance of those looks made so much more sense if they were all aware of the details of his situation.

"No one cares."

"They were all staring at me tonight."

"Because you maxed out the auction, got knocked up by one of the wealthiest men in the nation, disappeared for the duration, and showed back up with the prettiest damn baby they've ever seen who is sleeping in a fucking cardboard box!"

Adrien snorted. "Well, when you put it that way…"

"Yeah. Adrien, you have to go back to your alpha."

Adrien took his glasses off to rub at his eyes. "What about that Bluebeard story you told me?"

Lance choked on a laugh. "Does he have a secret room you can't look in? Did you uncover a bunch of skeletons of dead omegas?"

Adrien snorted. "Just the one." Lance hooted and then collapsed against the mattress laughing. "It's not funny."

"It's hilarious, friend!"

"How? He was in love with my omega parent. Was with him for years! Never told me about it! He says Nathan was cruel and unkind and…I don't even know how Nathan died! What if Heath killed him?"

"Do you really think he killed the man he loved?"

"Crimes of passion are real, Lance. Bluebeard—"

"Forget I told you that damn story. You're not living in some creepy old fairy tale, all right?" He sat up, entirely sober now. "Nathan died of a heart flaw."

Adrien replaced his glasses, sighing as Lance came into focus again. "How do you know?"

"The nephew is blabbing all the details of everything to everyone. We all know he died from a heart problem."

"My omega parent was a terrible person," Adrien murmured, his glasses slipping down his nose, and tears welling in his eyes.

"Ah, no, friend. From what you've said and what I've learned, Nathan was a heartbreaker and a rebellious omega, but so what? That doesn't mean he was a terrible person. He didn't follow the rules of society or our culture or *your* father's faith. But that doesn't mean he wasn't lovable. Your alpha loved him enough to want to breed with you for a piece of the man he'd cared for, a legacy of him."

"What if that's all I am to him?"

"You're the omega parent of his child. You're a loving, generous man." Lance frowned. "You're stuck in your head, babe, and you need to get out of it."

"But he loved Nathan. He was so dashing. I can't explain it. I just know I can't compare."

"Everything I hear about Nathan reminds me of my own omega parent, the one who left to go travel and never married my dad? All my dad's other omegas say he was selfish, but I think he just wanted to be free. It sounds to me that Heath wanted a more traditional relationship, and Nathan didn't. But they loved each other in their own way." Lance pointed his still half-full pint at Adrien. "But Heath could have a traditional relationship with you. You've never been one to push the envelope or want to go on great adventures. You might never have left the farm if your father hadn't died, for fear of breaking his heart."

"I'd have left the farm," Adrien said. "I'm not as boring as all that."

"I didn't say you were boring. I'm saying you're a simple man."

Adrien closed his eyes, remembering the joy he took in the garden, in the way the light moved down the tunnel of the nest, and he nodded. He didn't want all of this angst and hurtful suspicion. He wanted his peace back.

"Have you called him?"

He shrugged. "I let his old nurse Simon know we were safe."

"So Heath Clearwater knows where you are?"

Adrien sighed. "No. I thought he might try to come get us. I said we'd arrange a visit soon."

"He's got to be out of his mind worried about you both." Lance sipped from his bottle and then went on, the tart scent of apple drifting to Adrien on his breath. "Alphas get that way. He's got his own parental instincts, too, you know. He needs his baby near him. And his omega. He's probably going gray from the anxiety."

Adrien's gut wrenched imagining Heath in pain. "Thanks for supporting me in my difficult-as-hell situation, Lance," Adrien barked, shoving that softness down. "Glad to know you think this is all so fucking easy, and this is all in my crazy, messed up head."

"Whoa." Lance put his hands up. "Calm down. It's gonna be okay."

Michael farted again and started to fuss. Adrien picked him up and checked his diaper. His little bottom was a bit red, but he was still clean. He decided to change him anyway and moved over to the changing area he'd set up. He had hand sanitizer, but he wished there was a sink in the room.

Lance clucked his tongue.

"You think I've made a mistake?"

"I think you are letting that baby sleep in a *cardboard box.*"

"You're not going to let that go, are you?"

"Look. You can't stay here. This place isn't for babies, and it isn't for you. If you won't go back to him, then come home with me. My new apartment has a guest room with a bathroom attached. And a kitchen. And I'll borrow a crib from my parents' house. No one's pregnant right now, thank God."

"Wait, so when you say omega step-parents, you mean you have more than one right now?"

"Polyamory. Look it up."

As Adrien changed Michael's diaper, he made up his mind.

Lance was right. He needed to go back to Heath, work things out. Not only because he loved Heath and the dream of the future he'd nursed while pregnant in the nest, but also for Michael's sake. A baby deserved both of his parents, and his father's mistake made out of confusion and misguided love shouldn't prevent him from having that. Trust would need to be earned again, but that was still possible. There would be time.

Michael was all greased up below and in a new diaper when a mighty thump fell on the door. Both of them jumped. Lance's eyes went wide. "Holy shit," he gasped, looking around like he wanted to find a place to hide the pints. "You didn't think he'd come looking for you here? It's not like he didn't know where you used to live."

Another thump, and then Heath's voice. "I just need to see Michael." Then another loud thump. "Please, Adrien. I know you're in there. I can hear you."

Adrien grabbed Michael to his chest, opened the door, and found Heath looking haggard as hell. His beard was wild and his eyes bright. He took in the sight of Adrien and sagged in relief against the door. "And Michael?" he asked.

"Right here," Adrien said, indicating the baby in his arms.

Heath reached out and touched the baby's cheek. Then he nodded. "Okay. All right. Can I talk to you or should I go?"

"Stay," Adrien said before he'd fully made up his mind that was even what he wanted. "Come in. See Michael."

A small crowd had gathered in the hallway. The resident assistant called out, "Everything okay, Adrien?"

"We're fine."

The RA gave a thumbs-up. "Just shout if you need help."

"We're okay."

Lance was standing with both pints behind his back, like Heath was their father and they were drinking underage. "I'm gonna just—" He nodded at the door. "You cool?"

"I'm cool." Adrien was surprised it was true. Somehow just seeing Heath, all rumpled and exhausted, soothed him. Made him feel strong enough to handle this.

Lance cleared his throat but nodded. "Okay. Remember what I said about that baby."

"He's too pretty for the box. I know."

Lance slinked around Heath like he was afraid Heath might throw a punch, and maybe that would have been a risk if Heath didn't look like he'd gone a few rounds with himself already and had no strength to do anything but stare with wide, miserable, hungry eyes at Adrien and the baby.

"Can I hold him?" Heath asked, reaching out for Michael as soon as the door was shut behind Lance.

Adrien passed him over, his heart aching in all kinds of ways as Heath pressed kisses to the top of the baby's head and his fat cheeks. "He's okay, see?"

Heath breathed the baby in, and then he turned to Adrien. "And you? Are you okay?"

Adrien huffed. "No. I miss you. I haven't even gone to class or my office in the art department because I don't know what to do with Michael, and I don't know what I'm even doing here."

"And I don't know what I'm doing without you. Adrien, I made a terrible mistake. I'm so sorry."

"I forgive you."

Heath took a sharp breath. "Excuse me?"

"You said you made a terrible mistake and apologized. I forgive you."

"Just like that?"

"No, there's more I'll need from you over time, but, Heath…" Adrien took off his glasses, rubbed at his eyes, and put them back on again. "I see you clearly now. You chose me at the auction, and this time I choose you."

Heath stared at him. "Why?"

Adrien bit into his lower lip and stepped closer, his hands itching to touch. He let them rest on Heath's hips. "You loved Nathan so much you bought me to try to have a piece of him back. If you love me even half as much—"

"More. I love you more."

Adrien shook his head. "No, you don't. Not yet. And that's okay. You *will* love me more. Because I'm going to be everything Nathan wasn't. I'm going to be the man who you come home to, the man who raises your children, and the man who holds your hand in old age. I'm going to have you in every mood, every season. I will get to have every minute he gave up while he was out on his adventures, being 'free.' And you're going to prove that we were right to trust you, my omega parent and me."

"How?"

"You're going to love me forever."

"Yes. I promise." Heath reached out to him, hands trembling, and gray eyes soft with want. "Come home."

"To the nest?"

"To wherever. We don't have to live there," he said pleadingly. "I'll make a home wherever you want. Build any house you want, designed just for you, anywhere in the fifteen nations. I just want to be with you."

"What if I want us to stay here? In the dorm?" Adrien didn't want that at all, but he wanted to push just to see what Heath would do.

Heath's eyes darted to the cardboard box crib. "We should aim a little higher than here. But otherwise, anywhere."

Adrien laughed, and it shocked him that he could. "Lance wasn't impressed with my setup either."

"Who's Lance?"

"My friend. The guy who just left?"

"Oh. Him. Right." Heath kissed Michael some more before closing his eyes and reaching out for Adrien again, almost like he couldn't bear to watch Adrien reject him. His sigh when Adrien stepped into his arms was more like a sob.

"I've always wanted to see the beach," Adrien whispered.

"We can live there if that's what you want," Heath said, voice straining with emotion.

"I was already going to come home, you know."

Heath shook in his arms, saying nothing.

"I'm not like Nathan. I hated being away from you."

Heath clung to him hard, and Michael squirmed between them.

"From now on, you'll be honest with me. No more secrets." Adrien breathed in Heath's warm, familiar scent. He smelled like he might not have bathed in a few days. He smelled like he was desperate and in love. "Not even for, like, a surprise party. Zero secrets."

"I promise."

"And to that effect I have to confess something."

"All right."

"I'm glad you bid on me because I was Nathan's son. I'm grateful because I love you, and because now we have Michael."

"Thank you."

"I also have one question and one thing you must know."

Heath nodded, holding him close. "Okay."

"Nathan died of a heart flaw. Could I have it? Could Michael?" Adrien's blood zipped quickly, and he met Heath's eyes, reading them. "Be honest."

"I promise. You and Michael are safe from it. It was a flaw from overuse. He had abused some powders that gave him extra energy at times. The doctors said it wasn't congenital."

Adrien nodded sharply. "Thank you. I needed to hear that. I've been worried." He cleared his throat. "Now, you have to know—I want to do more with my life than make babies all the time. I want to have a career in studying material art."

"All right."

"But I do want to make babies *some* of the time."

Heath laughed, a sobbing huff against Adrien's hair. "You make beautiful ones."

"And I like being pregnant."

"Will you want to return to the heat cabin? Or should I think about having somewhere else prepared?"

"Let's wait until I'm closer to my next heat. Then we can decide."

"Yes." Heath said it like a prayer of thanks. "So you will marry me?"

"I will. But in the meantime, I want you to take me away from here. I'm tired, and I want to be home."

"To the nest?"

"Please." Adrien nuzzled Heath's neck, the baby squirming between them. "Where you can take care of me and command me. Where you're the alpha, and I'm your omega."

Heath straightened, standing tall. "Then let's go home, little one."

# Epilogue

HEATH SAID THE house they built by the sea was much homier than the castle had ever been. He had a nest area added on to it, too. Four cozy and breezy rooms where Adrien could ruminate and grow their next child, but not quite so isolated from the rest of the house this time, so that Michael would always have access to his omega parent.

Adrien hated to leave their fresh, beautiful home for the week, but he also knew the comforts of the new nest would be waiting for him when they got back.

The heat cabin was exactly the way Adrien remembered it, small and set deep into the woods. But this time, he approached it with a light step and expectation. This was his choice and his life. A second child to be Michael's younger sibling, hopefully a better one than Lidell had been to Heath, and then Adrien would return to school until he finished his research. They'd consider a third child at that point if Adrien wanted one.

"Show me your hole," Heath said as they climbed out of the car. The winter air was chill, and Adrien shivered. "So I know what I paid for."

Adrien laughed. He stripped down and shoved his clothes and glasses back into the car. He wouldn't be needing them. Then he turned around, bent over the warm hood, cold air on his back and heat spreading over his front. He pulled his ass cheeks wide. "Do you like it?" he asked, a flutter of embarrassment in his chest. He was still unsure about his body after the first pregnancy and birth, but Heath couldn't seem to get enough.

"That's my gorgeous slutty man," Heath muttered. "Oh, little one, I'm going to knot you so hard."

"I'm counting on it," Adrien said, as Heath moved in behind him, knelt on the ground, and began to tongue his asshole hungrily. He reached back with one hand and gripped Heath's hair, dragging him in closer to get more. "Oh, yes. Fuck me."

"You want me? Here? Now?" Heath asked, coming up for breath, licking his way from Adrien's tailbone to his shoulder blade and then kissing his neck.

"Yes."

"Beg me for it."

"Knot me, please. Fill me up with your child. I want it. I need it."

"You beg so prettily. It's a good thing I've got this right here"—he unzipped his pants—"to help you out."

Adrien's eyes rolled back in his head as Heath slid home, fucking into him with a quick, eager thrust, made easy by the copious slick Adrien had produced on the ride up. He shoved his ass back, grinding on Heath's cock, gloating that it was so thick, so hard, and already pulsing in his ass. He loved this man, he loved the life they were making together: traditional and yet full of fun, love, and respect.

"Fill me up," he whispered. "Knot me."

Heath shuddered and whispered in his ear, "I love you. Only you."

Adrien worked his asshole around Heath's cock and was rewarded by Heath biting down on his shoulder, groaning, and spurting into his gut. The fat girth of the growing knot kept him pinned against the car, and they both laughed at their predicament.

"Hope you like this position," Heath said. "We're going to be here awhile." Heath took off his jacket, jostling the knot, and draped it on Adrien's back to keep him warm, before laying down over him.

Caught between the warmth of the car hood and the heat of Heath's body, Adrien was content to be pinned in place, convulsing in pleasure, for as long as it took. "I'll be happy anywhere so long as I'm with you," he whimpered.

Heath nuzzled his neck, wrapped his arms around him, and murmured, "Me, too, little one. Me, too."

Their love story had just begun.

THE END

If you'd like to read more in the Heat for Sale universe, please pick up Bully for Sale.
https://mybook.to/bullypreorder

## Letter from Leta Blake

Dear Reader,

If you're looking for more in this universe, check out Bully for Sale.

If you enjoyed the book, please take a moment to leave a review! Reviews not only help readers determine if a book is for them, but also help a book show up in searches.

The absolute best way to keep up with me is to join my newsletter. I send one out on average once per week. There you'll find all my upcoming news and information on releases.

Also I'd love if you followed me at BookBub or Goodreads to be notified of new releases and deals. To see some sources of my inspiration, you can follow my Pinterest boards.

And look for me on Facebook or Instagram for snippets of the day-to-day writing life, or join my Facebook Group for announcements and special giveaways.

For the audiobook connoisseur, several of my Leta Blake books are available at most retailers which sell audio, all performed by skilled and talented narrators. Look for me on Audible.

Thank you so much for being a reader!
Leta Blake

*Another book in the Heat for Sale universe*

## BULLY FOR SALE

by Leta Blake

**Heat can be sold, but love is earned.**

Bullied and outcast, Ezer has seen firsthand the cruelties of the world. He knows what's expected from his kind—timid compliance and submission to his "betters." But Ezer isn't one to roll over and conform to the role society has forced upon him.

Despite his defiant nature, Ezer is coerced into partnering with a man of his father's choosing. One his father promises will love and care for him for the rest of his life.

A night of nameless and faceless passion later, Ezer is horrified to find himself bound to Ned, a bully who has done so much to make his life hell. Ezer's determined to hate Ned but he can't help the way his body craves his touch.

Ned is young, privileged, and hopelessly in love with Ezer. Too bad his pack of so-called "friends" have targeted Ezer for torment. Ned has a lot of regrets, but none greater than his role in Ezer's misery. When Ned's offered the contract of a lifetime, he sees it as the only way forward with the man he loves.

The dual biological drives of heat and its aftermath might be all that's keeping them close now, but Ned is determined to prove he's worthy of Ezer's love. While Ezer is just as determined not to fall for his bully.

*Bully for Sale* is a standalone m/m romance set in the *Heat for Sale* universe featuring a redemption story, forced proximity, first times, bully romance, opposites attract, and enemies to lovers.

**Content Warnings:** bullying, family coercion, family emotional manipulation and abuse, difficult pregnancy and birth, consent violations due to family coercion, sexual assault (not between the heroes), knotting, mpreg, omegaverse.

*Book One in the Heat of Love series*

## SLOW HEAT

by Leta Blake

**A lustful young alpha meets his match in an older omega with a past.**

Professor Vale Aman has crafted a good life for himself. An unbonded omega in his mid-thirties, he's long since given up hope that he'll meet a compatible alpha, let alone his destined mate. He's fulfilled by his career, his poetry, his cat, and his friends.

When Jason Sabel, a much younger alpha, imprints on Vale in a shocking and public way, longings are ignited that can't be ignored. Fighting their strong sexual urges, Jason and Vale must agree to contract with each other before they can consummate their passion.

But for Vale, being with Jason means giving up his independence and placing his future in the hands of an untested alpha—as well as facing the scars of his own tumultuous past. He isn't sure it's worth it. But Jason isn't giving up his destined mate without a fight.

This is a gay romance novel, 118,000 words, with a strong happy ending, as well as a well-crafted, **non-shifter** omegaverse, with alphas, betas, omegas, male pregnancy, heat, and **knotting**. Content warning for pregnancy loss and aftermath.

*Standalone*

## ANY GIVEN LIFETIME

by Leta Blake

**He'll love him in any lifetime.**

Neil isn't a ghost, but he feels like one. Reincarnated with all his memories from his prior life, he spent twenty years trapped in a child's body, wanting nothing more than to grow up and reclaim the love of his life.

As an adult, Neil finds there's more than lost time separating them. Joshua has built a beautiful life since Neil's death, and how exactly is Neil supposed to introduce himself? As Joshua's long-dead lover in a new body? Heartbroken and hopeless, Neil takes refuge in his work, developing microscopic robots called nanites that can produce medical miracles.

When Joshua meets a young scientist working on a medical project, his soul senses something his rational mind can't believe. Has Neil truly come back to him after twenty years? And if the impossible is real, can they be together at long last?

*Any Given Lifetime* is a stand-alone, slow burn, second chance gay romance by Leta Blake featuring reincarnation and true love. This story includes some angst, some steam, an age gap, and, of course, a happy ending.

*Standalone*

# THE RIVER LEITH

by Leta Blake

**Amnesia stole his memories, but it can't erase their love.**

Leith is terrified after waking up in a hospital bed to find his most recent memories are three years out of date.

Worse, he can't even remember how he met the beautiful man who visits him most days. Everyone claims Zach is his best friend, but Leith's feelings for Zach aren't friendly.

They're so much more than that.

Zach fills Leith with longing. Attraction. Affection. **Lust**. And those feelings are even scarier than losing his memory, because Leith's always been straight. Hasn't he?

For Zach, being forgotten by his lover is excruciating. Leith's amnesia has stolen everything: their relationship, their happiness, and the man he loves. Suddenly single and alone, Zach knows nothing will ever be okay again.

Desperate to feel better, Zach confesses his grief to the faceless Internet. But his honesty might come back to haunt them both.

*The River Leith* is a standalone MM romance with amnesia trope, hurt/comfort, bisexual discovery, "first time" gay scenes, a second chance at first love, and a satisfying happy ending.

# Other Books by Blake Moreno

## Contemporary

Will & Patrick Wake Up Married
Will & Patrick's Endless Honeymoon
Cowboy Seeks Husband
The Difference Between
Bring on Forever
Stay Lucky

**Sports**

The River Leith

*The Training Season Series*
Training Season
Training Complex

**Musicians**

Smoky Mountain Dreams
Vespertine

**New Adult**

Punching the V-Card

**Winter Holidays**

*The Home for the Holidays Series*
Mr. Frosty Pants
Mr. Naughty List
Mr. Jingle Bells

## Fantasy

Any Given Lifetime

**Re-imagined Fairy Tales**

Flight
Levity

**Paranormal & Shifters**

Angel Undone
Omega Mine

**Horror**

Raise Up Heart

## Omegaverse

*Heat of Love Series*
Slow Heat
Alpha Heat
Slow Birth
Bitter Heat

*For Sale Series*
Heat for Sale
Bully for Sale

## Coming of Age

*'90s Coming of Age Series*
Pictures of You
You Are Not Me

## Audiobooks

Leta Blake at Audible

## Discover more about the author online

Leta Blake
letablake.com

## Gay Romance Newsletter

Leta's newsletter will keep you up to date on her latest releases and news from the world of M/M romance. Join the mailing list today and you're automatically entered into future giveaways.

## Leta Blake on Patreon

Become part of Leta Blake's Patreon community in order to access exclusive content, deleted scenes, extras, bonus stories, rewards, prizes, interviews, and more.
www.patreon.com/letablake

# About the Author

Author of the bestselling book Smoky Mountain Dreams and the fan favorite Training Season, Leta Blake's educational and professional background is in psychology and finance, respectively. However, her passion has always been for writing. She enjoys crafting romance stories and exploring the psyches of made up people. At home in the Southern U.S., Leta works hard at achieving balance between her day job, her writing, and her family.

Made in the USA
Monee, IL
30 January 2024

52630566R00142